Unlucky or Not

Wendy Hughes Hare

Blackstone Editions
Toronto, Ontario, Canada
www.BlackstoneEditions.com

Second printing: April 2018

978-0-9816402-7-3

Edited by Anne Rawson and Jan Melnyk
Cover design by Logan Hughes

This book is dedicated to all women who struggle with their body image and imperfections. Wendy's story encourages us to embrace and celebrate our uniqueness.

Much of this tale is set in an area of Ontario that the author loved. It was fueled by the inspiration of her children, Sam and Bronwen, her loving husband Wayne, and her extended family.

Born on August 28, 1956, Wendy succumbed to her battle with cancer at her home in Port Hope, Ontario, lovingly surrounded by her family and her cherished dog, Penny. She was a talented and creative soul and a blessing to everyone who knew her.

Robert,

Happy Retirement!

I hope that even
with your theatre
duties you will find
the time to read my
sister's book.

Cheers!

Bill

Prologue

According to family legend, my mother picked my name out of the obituaries. The story goes that, while skimming the birth notices for possibilities, her eye slipped down the page to the death notices and landed on Penelope-Marie. She circled the name with a red pencil and made the announcement to my father. Glancing up from the sports section, he nodded, and that was that.

My mother had a vivid imagination and was an insatiable reader. Books were stacked on every table and shelf of our house. She loved rummaging through second-hand stores, buying bushels of books. She was forever suggesting that I read her latest find. Frequently I found tomato seeds or mustard smeared across a page or two. She read while cooking, eating, and walking. Dad even accused her of doing so while driving. Especially the day she ended up in a ditch on Butter and Egg Road.

I remember the summer she purchased a bulky novel called *The Women's Room* by Marilyn French. She became so absorbed, she served us cold cereal for ten consecutive meals. My brother and I were ready to re-enact *Mutiny on the Bounty*. We called Dad at the restaurant and he brought home chicken souvlaki and Greek salad.

During her second pregnancy she became so enamoured with Hemingway's *The Old Man and the Sea* that she named my baby brother Marlin. She said it was a perfect moniker given that he landed into the world weighing a solid ten pounds two ounces.

They say the apple doesn't fall far from the tree. One morning, when my mother was preoccupied with my baby brother, I scribbled the words — CAT, TIGGER, SEEGULL, MONKEE — all over the living room walls with markers. Because I had sounded the words out phonetically, my mother recognised my talent and captured it with her trusty instamatic camera.

My father, however, didn't share her enthusiasm. From that day forward, he brought home a stack of take-out-burger newsprint from the restaurant. I spent hours folding and stapling the newsprint into books. My novels were scattered all over — with titles like *Mom and the Moon People* and *The Big Surprise*. The latter describes, splat by splat, how my baby brother pooped during nap time and then created a Jackson Pollock-like painting by tossing the content of his diaper all over the room.

I objected to my brother's entrance into the universe. I was only two but I remember that day clearly. My father parked our minivan at the front door of the hospital. I was astonished when he didn't unstrap me from my car seat. Instead, he opened the passenger door. I turned my head and saw my mother being rolled toward us in a wheelchair. I watched in shock as a nurse helped my dad secure a blue parcel into another car seat beside me. Then the blanket started to bawl. In turn, I screamed and couldn't stop. My mother ordered my father to pull the car into the parking lot at the Mac's Milk store. He raced inside and bought a Jetsicle. She claimed the ice cream was a present from my new brother, AKA the blue wailing lump. I stopped howling. However, two days later, after biding my time—generous in my estimation—I made a simple request. Digging the car keys out of my mother's handbag, I asked her to take the alien back to the hospital.

The animosity I shared with my younger and only sibling soon faded, however. We figured out we were more alike than not. He was the first to call me Pen—in grade school, I had tucked an HB pencil behind my ear and always had a Hilroy exercise book in hand. The smell of the pencil sharpener was nirvana to my senses. By high school, I had graduated to Staedtler pens and pocket-size black Moleskine notebooks, which I shoved into the pouch of my backpack. I always jotted down the goofy things Marlin and his friends said. It drove them nuts. Late at night, I'd scribble away in my room, listening to Leonard Cohen and Bruce Cockburn, writing poetry and imagining myself the Sylvia Plath of Monck Township.

The other indispensable member of our family was our dog Ziska. My brother and I had found her riffling through debris at the local landfill. She jumped into our car and that was it! In no time she doubled her weight and took over the house. Her ears were her trademark—in Zen-like moments they stuck out sideways, like Yoda's.

My childhood was punctuated by illness and accidents. From the day I was prematurely born, I succeeded in picking up every possible childhood illness. Any infection—croup, scarlet fever, whooping cough—I contracted them all. In Grade Eight, to my supreme horror, I was hospitalized with mononucleosis, the kissing disease. I couldn't swallow, my throat was so swollen. Rumours flared like a grease fire when I returned to school ten days later. No one would sit within two desks of me.

As for accidents, they began the day I learned to walk; apparently, I wobbled past my mother's open arms and fell over my father's foot, slicing my lip open on the corner of the coffee table. Five stitches. It was therefore no surprise when, years later, in the middle of my brother's sixth birthday party, I crashed my bike into a tree and broke my arm in two places. The party was instantly dissolved, and Marlin was fuming mad.

My illnesses and frequent accidents were really inconsequential, though. For me, the real albatross was my unsightliness. My ears and nose had grown too quickly. I had my dad's nose, bookended by large ears that protruded between thin wisps of red hair. I tried to ignore the grade-school ogres who revelled in teasing me. But one day, in Grade Three, the teacher left the room to take Polly McFadden to the nurse's office with her twelfth nosebleed of the week. When I opened my desk and grabbed my math scribbler, I found a gift-wrapped box. My heart pounded. Who knew it was my birthday? I remember unwrapping the pink tissue while the whole class watched. As I opened the box, my stomach lurched. There, facing me, was a dog collar. Engraved in large letters was the name *Unlucky*. One of the boys started to bark, and the classroom erupted in laughter.

That's when it started. The cringing. The hiding. The crouching. At recess, I would disappear behind a fence, scribbling in my notebook. At lunch I buried myself nose-deep in a book. If an author described a main character as pleasing to the eye, I'd slam the book shut. If the protagonist had a stutter or warts, I'd read on recklessly. I loved Pippi Longstocking and devoured all three books. If only I had her strength as well as her red hair; red hair alone made you a sitting duck.

I dreaded the MacKenzie sisters. The older one was in my grade, and the other was in Marlin's class. After the dog collar incident, the two sisters growled at me whenever we crossed paths. When I pleaded with them to stop, they'd only woof louder.

They lived in the most ostentatious house in town, like a life-size Fisher-Price medieval castle. I decided they were demon princesses and was not fooled, as others were, by their angelic smiles. One recess, they cornered me behind a snowbank. Almost spitting in my face, they explained to me that if you're a cute baby, you become an ugly child, and if you're a hideous kid—spit—you become a good-looking adult. The older one yanked off my toque, causing my hair to stick straight up with static, her lip curling into a sneer. With her nose inches from mine she declared: "If that's the case, you're going to be one heck of a beauty."

The next morning over breakfast my brother enthusiastically shared news of my ordeal. My mother dropped her paperback and bolted from her chair, searching for the car keys. Attaching myself to her leg, I pleaded, "Please, please don't go to the school." I was smart enough to know that if she talked to the principal, the abuse would multiply exponentially. She reluctantly agreed as long as I promised to tell her of any future incident. Later that night, when we were brushing our teeth, I remember thrusting my seven-year-old brother up against the tiled bathroom wall and making him swear not to utter another word about the MacKenzie sisters.

Unlucky. It was the nickname whispered, chanted, and shouted at me on a daily basis in the schoolyard. The memories still flicker in my head, a moving picture of my classmates' twisted mouths, their faces sneering, as they yelled: "Here, Unlucky, fetch! Fetch the ball!" The ball then being tossed high in the air and their harsh laughter ricocheting off the brick walls.

It was my nemesis.

Part One

The Night That Changed My Life

One

I didn't see it coming—even with the binoculars. I should have, since one of my favourite John Lennon lyrics was about life kicking you in the butt when you least expect it.

I had persuaded myself I was living the dream. Everything that didn't fit inside my illusion, I had carefully archived like artifacts in a subterranean vault.

As I perched like a raven, fifty feet up in a tree, fingers clenched like claws on a branch, my world was about to unravel.

I declined to call it snooping. After all, why should the architect of the stag be banned from attending? Who makes the rules for prenuptial celebrations anyway? Brooding over Boyd's bachelor party would normally have been the last thing on my mind. I found the whole tradition mind-numbing. But as planner, I really felt I deserved the pleasure of watching my victim squirm. Boyd, the fiancé of my best friend Kim, had been bucking for this retaliation.

Two years before, he had typed a note on letterhead pilfered from the high school. It declared that there had been a computer glitch. I would have to return and make up two more credits—including a compulsory machine shop course. Not finishing high school was my recurring nightmare. Upon receiving the registered letter, I had freaked out. I hysterically dialled the school office, confused the bejesus out of the secretary and demanded to speak to the principal. I kicked myself afterwards. The shop course should have been a dead giveaway. Boyd has never let me live it down.

Prior to the night of the stag, my brother Marlin had lectured me. "Repeat after me: I, Penelope-Marie Papadopoulos, do solemnly promise not to show up at the party." I laughed. I hadn't even told my boyfriend, Jake, that I had helped organize the stag. First of all, he would be there and secondly, he was old school so I knew he would probably hit the roof.

Earlier, I had jotted down possible things I could do on the evening of the party, rather than check out the festivities. Some would say list-making makes you a crock-a-block neurotic. But as a writer, I believe in recording everything — then marking off accomplishments. Check. Check. Check. Complete.

- Go to bed early to catch up on missed hours of sleep. (*Nope. Boring. I'm in my twenties, not nineties.*)
- Extract all the Tim Horton's coffee cups out of the car and detail the dash with Armour All and Q-tips. (*Double nope.*)
- Bathe the dog.
- ~~Start a novel. Start a novelette.~~ Start a short story.
- Think up a good idea for a blog.
- Organize the kitchen cupboards. A to Z.

In retrospect, I should have stayed home, tackled my list and watched *The Accidental Tourist* for the seventh time.

The bald tires on my Cavalier rumbled as they crossed the bridge past the falls. I rarely noticed the view, hardly Niagara, but most outsiders thought it impressive. The rushing, churning water had become familiar to me.

I wondered about the time and glanced at the dash only to remember that the radio and clock had burst into flames last year, the clock forever stuck on 11:11. Thankfully, the windshield wipers still worked on my beat-up two-door hatchback. This rust-bucket was my freedom; there's no public transit in Bracebridge, unless you count Santa's trolley. Ding, ding.

Whatever. I loved my town. It was the Vermont of Ontario, with rock cuts the colour of rare prime rib. In fall, riffraff motored helter-skelter in SUVs. Braking abruptly, they'd lean out their windows with long-lens Nikons to capture red and gold maples. In summer, Toronto crowds and cottagers arrived to soak up the sun. They propelled jet skis in tight circles on lakes and yanked every last box of Honey Nut Cheerios from store shelves. On rainy summer days, they cruised downtown, stalked our streets, licked butter tart ice cream cones and sipped low fat lattes. For us locals, it was teeth gnashing time. Traffic stood still and you could count on waiting through two traffic lights just to turn onto main street. Tourists! Unfortunately, these outsiders were also a mega source of revenue, creating jobs like my father's.

Boyd's bachelor party had been scheduled to begin at 8:00 p.m. at Kim's house, but this group was always late. I knew I wouldn't miss the main attraction, but I was anxious to find the perfect spot for my stakeout. I turned right onto Beaumont Drive, opposite the route I usually barrelled down on the north side of the Muskoka River. My eyes diverted to landmarks across the water. My tires momentarily drifted from the pavement, spraying gravel. I quickly turned the steering wheel, bumping back onto the road.

I had been organizing Kim's wedding shower when my party planning itch had taken over. I had been seduced by all the lists and priorities. I'd opened my big mouth and offered to help the guys with the bachelor party. We'd met for drinks and, in a beer-infused moment, the plan was hatched.

I pulled into the driveway of the boarded-up cottage just across the river from Kim's place. It seemed an ideal spot for viewing the stag. Like many of the river cottages, the owner had a right-of-way to a strip of land along the waterway next to the road. I crossed the pavement, stepping onto their floating pier. Damn. The view was too restrictive. I could only see the flag flying atop Kim's boathouse. Hearing voices across the water, I hopped back onto the bank and sprinted down the road. Through a curtain of hemlocks, I saw flashes of the first guests arriving. As I shoved the boughs aside to gain a better vantage point, thorns the size of fish hooks ripped into my hand. Falling backwards, I tripped on a huge root and landed flat on my back. When I looked up, there was a majestic white pine towering overhead. Found. One ideal lookout point. Yes, it would be perfect!

I quickly returned to the car and yanked my knapsack from the passenger seat. Inside was a thermos of coffee, a flashlight, a square of baklava, a fork, a napkin, a variety of fine-tipped pens, mechanical pencils and my notebook. *Be Prepared* was my motto. Then I remembered my brother's binoculars. In the trunk, I shoved aside a box of rocks, welder's goggles, a cowbell, a handsaw and a broken fishing rod and extracted a tattered leather case.

Luckily, I had left Ziska, my dog and keenest companion, at home. She loves car rides but wouldn't have appreciated being tied to a tree. With her stubborn streak she'd most likely scream like a banshee. It's the same sound she makes when I can't throw the ball fast enough. Ear-splitting!

Returning to the base of the pine, I kicked off my clunky sandals and gripped the lower branch. Using momentum, and trying to avoid the tree sap, I lunged upward from one branch to the next. I landed lightly on a limb that felt spongy under my feet. Geez, I've got to be careful. The sun was setting and I blinked as the rays of light criss-crossed my face. I continued up the tree. When I reached a point where the view of Kim's dock became clear, I rested on a branch, holding on for dear life.

When I was two, I used to hook my arms around my mother's neck. She had called me her little monkey. Here I was, twenty years later, hugging a white pine, forty feet up in the air. It had been over a decade since I'd last climbed a tree. For a moment, gazing out across the river, I actually felt serene. The wind had settled. The boats that whizzed up and down during the day were tied up at docks or bobbing in boat slips. Although I had a slight dread of heights, the exhilaration of the view momentarily outweighed my fear.

I tried to get comfortable. I clung onto the trunk with one arm and gripped a bulky branch with my other hand, squatting and sitting carefully, my legs dangling. I wriggled out of my backpack and hung it beside me, extracting my pen and my trusty Moleskine notebook. It would be a challenge making notes while simultaneously peering through binoculars.

A horsefly, one of the fat, nasty, rip-out-a-chunk-of-flesh kinds, buzzed my head, stirring me from my contemplation.

It landed fleetingly on my knee. I whacked at it with my notebook—and missed. It approached again and momentarily I forgot where I was, raising my hand as if brandishing a sword. Regaining my balance, I grabbed the trunk again, squirmed and dropped my favourite pen. The Pigma Micron 02 scuttled through the branches below into the twilight. Oh, no! I loved that pen.

I sighed and shoved the notebook back into my knapsack pocket, then peered through the binoculars. The pier in front of Kim's place was expansive. If the Queen Mary had sailed up the Muskoka River, it could have easily tied up to this quay. Slowly, the dock filled up with men—if you could call these overgrown post-adolescents *men*. The libations began to flow and their voices grew louder. From across the river, I couldn't make out what they were saying, but I imagined the conversation. Customary male jocularity: bragging about their prowess with broads, the swiftness of their muscle Ford F-150s, or how much money they'd won on the Pro-Line sports lottery. I moved the field glasses to the left, honing in on the corner of the boathouse. No one seemed to have noticed the bulky object wrapped in a tarp, tucked under the eaves. Perfect.

Pop. Unexpectedly the dock lights illuminated. I had been fixated on the action and hadn't realized that the sun was sinking below the horizon. Hearing a familiar shout, I swung the binoculars to the right and focused on the path across the river. I recognized the swagger of my boyfriend, Jake, as he ambled towards the shore.

Two

The first time I had laid eyes on Jake he was wearing white gymnastic tights. His posture was like a soldier on parade. My Grade Eleven gym teacher had forced our class to watch an interschool competition. Sitting on the top bleacher, I had pulled out my history text to cram for a quiz. When I glanced up, I became mesmerized by this broad-shouldered hunk rubbing chalk on his hands. His sandy hair, square chin and sculptured body were to die for.

I couldn't stop staring. He jumped to grab the high bar, swinging his legs, kipping his waist parallel to the bar. Then, rotating at his hips, he dropped, falling into a forward giant swing, his arms extended, his body revolving. His hands squeezed the bar. His muscles rippled. I held my breath. He was spinning so fast, I was sure he'd fly off and slam into the wall. I had never noticed him before among the jokers in the high school halls or thought anyone in our school could possibly be so... talented.

I was simply agog. I told Kim "agog" was the perfect word to describe my mood. I had rarely allowed myself to even like boys. I was petrified of getting hurt, a throwback to being bullied in public school. But with Jake, I couldn't help myself. I talked about him incessantly, mumbling in divine rapture.

I started trolling every party in town looking for this mysterious young man. I had always despised teenage gatherings. Lumbering drunks. Dark basements or cold garages. A backdrop of raucous music. But I dragged myself to these events hoping to casually bump into him. No such luck.

Then, one Saturday night, at the most unlikely of places, I spotted him. I had been working the late shift at my father's restaurant and three boys had just stiffed me for the bill. I should have known better, as the delinquents had ordered the most expensive items on our menu—a steak sandwich and chocolate milkshake. I had turned my back to refill a customer's coffee cup, when suddenly I saw the scoundrels duck out. Slamming the pot down on the counter, I barrelled after them, crashing into Jake as he entered the restaurant.

"What's the problem?" he asked, grabbing me by the shoulders.

"Those idiots dined and dashed!" I retorted. My face was crimson as I pointed to the departing shadows.

He bolted out the door, returning minutes later with three twenty-dollar bills in his hand. "Will this cover it?" he asked. I nodded. He was dressed in dark jeans with a button-down baby-blue shirt. His hair fell over his eyes. A twentieth-century Apollo. I was too thunderstruck to speak and just nodded.

He then perched himself on the counter stool. When I handed him a menu, he asked, "Your name's Pen, right? I hear you are really smart." I was speechless. How did this dreamboat know my name? Beyond my wildest dreams, he stayed until the restaurant closed. He downed cup after cup of coffee, watching me serve tables. When it was slow, we chatted. About what, I don't remember. Around eleven, we were deluged with our classmates ordering mass quantities of chips and gravy. He picked up one of the gray plastic bins, bussing the tables, piling up the ketchup-splattered plates.

"Hey, Jake, when did you get a job here?" yelled a girl.

He continued swabbing down the table and smiled. "Just helping a friend." With that, I ducked into the kitchen and gave the bewildered cook a high-five.

Jake drove me home that night, flying across the flats, a strip of highway in the valley outside of town. Immersed in banter, he overshot my road by thirty minutes, hitting the outskirts of the village of Port Carling before either of us noticed. When he called the next day to ask me to a movie I acted nonchalant, but leapt wildly around the living room after hanging up.

From that point on we saw each other every weekend and, in no time, we were eating lunch together every day in the school cafeteria. We were a couple. I remember not believing it. I had a boyfriend. A very hot boyfriend. Girls seemed shocked and even jealous — how cool was that?

It irked me, however, that we were often viewed as mismatched socks. I could tell by the infuriating stares from girls and their "what-is-he-doing-with-her?" expressions. I tried not to pay attention. After all, he was traffic-stopping good-looking and any girl would feel insecure beside him. Right? Besides, every woman had her body issues. In addition to my nose, mine was my lower half, despite Kim's claim that I was utterly clueless about how bodacious my butt was.

After graduating from high school, we car-pooled to Georgian College, an hour drive south. Jake had enrolled in a computer course while I was earning a journalism diploma. Following college, his grandfather found him a job at the town hall and I became a junior writer at *The Bracebridge Bugle*. While many of our generation had already escaped to the big city, we settled into small town life. Everyone kept asking, "When are you going to get married?" Jake had been acting a little strange, which made me believe it must be on the tip of his tongue. Would I be able to spot the small blue velvet box from fifty paces?

Three

Refocusing with the binoculars, I could see that Jake was the only guest at the stag who had dressed for the occasion. He looked stunning in a perfectly-fitted black sports jacket, pressed khakis, and a crisp white t-shirt. Even after all these years, just looking at him made my heart flutter.

A flicker in the left lens startled me. Boyd, the groom-to-be, was thrashing around in the water. Here we go, I thought. The rowdiness had commenced. I prayed he'd survive the revelry without ending up tied to a tree, stark naked. His buddies were sadistic. When I had met with Kim's brother John and Boyd's pals to discuss the party, some of their ideas bordered on out-and-out depravity. First they would get him inebriated to the point of unconsciousness. Then they would throw him on a freight train to Sault Ste. Marie. My suggestion for the evening's plan seemed tame in comparison, but they all reluctantly agreed it might be fun.

I'd neglected to tell Kim about my involvement with the stag. Luckily, she'd been working the night shift at the hospital. In her opinion, the safest place to stage the party would be at her house. There would be no chance of any trouble at her place!

As I continued to watch, Boyd climbed up the ladder, jeans dripping. He then stripped down to his plaid jockey shorts and accepted another beer from John. In the background, I noticed Jake placing his folded pants onto the arm of a lounger. He stretched, flexed and then executed a perfect double handspring across the dock. Diving into the water, his toes flawlessly pointed, he scarcely left a ripple. The guys clapped and cheered. Jake was a sucker for an audience.

My hands ached. Slowly, I released my grip around the binoculars, letting them dangle around my neck as I wiggled my fingers. I pulled the thermos out of my backpack single-handedly and took a slurp of coffee. My stomach grumbled but I decided the sticky baklava would have to wait.

Within moments, I became aware of the first few dreamy notes of a familiar song floating across the river. The notes stopped and I smiled. That was the signal. Through the binoculars, I watched as John and my brother slipped away from the group. Together, the two pushed a covered box on rollers towards the middle of the wharf. It occurred to me how stuffy it must be curled up in that box waiting for the cue. At the last second, they whipped off the tarp and the speakers vibrated with Madonna's *Like a Virgin*.

Boyd wavered unsteadily on his feet. A beer bottle dangled from his hand. I zeroed in on his face. When he saw the pink and white wooden crate, his mouth was agape. His head turned from side to side. Bang! With that, the lid flew off and out popped a female, hands in the air. With the help of John, she stepped onto the dock, clad only in stilettos, a sparkly thong and pasties. She slithered towards the groom, hips undulating to the beat. I wondered how it was possible for her to prance about without catching a heel in the deck boards. Boyd stepped backwards. The look on his face was my reward; he was such an innocent! He would never be caught dead in a strip bar. This was cliché bachelor party entertainment, designed to thoroughly embarrass him. Gotcha!

His friends shoved him into a Muskoka chair. The dancer leaned on the wide arms, swinging her breasts in his face, and twirling her pasties. Everyone whistled and clapped. He struggled to stand up, but his buddies held him down. The stripper turned, bending and jiggling her butt.

I watched his face. His eyes were clamped shut. I slowly panned the binoculars across the dock. My brother was admiring his workmanship on the faux cake. Behind him, Jake stood alone in the shadows, his face obscured.

As the last notes of the song faded, the dancer stopped and the groom flew to his feet. He shook the girl's hand, ever the consummate gentleman, and escaped drunkenly to the house before anything else could happen. The stripper looked around uncomfortably, one hand on her hip, looking for her compensation. John, who'd hired her from a bar in Gravenhurst, stepped forward and handed her an envelope.

The joke had gone off without a hitch. It would go down in Bracebridge folklore. Payback for all Boyd's April Fools' pranks. I downed the last drip of coffee from my thermos in celebration.

Ouch! My butt was aching from sitting on the branch, but I took one final look. This is when I saw Jake saunter up to the lap dancer. I zoomed in. His lips were moving and her chin nodded. He slipped off his jacket and draped it over her shoulders. Meanwhile, someone turned up a Rush CD and guys began digging into the cooler for more beer. No one seemed to notice my boyfriend escorting the girl up the path. They lingered, standing under one of the path lights. What were they discussing so avidly? Jake offered her his beer bottle. She accepted, taking a long draught. Then I saw her lips move, and he replied, smiling slowly. The woman's head bobbed and I heard her high-pitched laughter ring across the river. She then sat down on a wooden bench, and Jake sat beside her. He pulled off one of her shoes and began to massage her foot. Wait a minute. What the heck did he think he was doing? I focused on her face. She looked like some Vegas show girl with luminescent blue eyeshadow and fake eyelashes. Her brassy blonde hair was tightly drawn into a ponytail, sprouting like a fountain off the top of her head. She leaned forward as if she might kiss him. I gasped, momentarily losing my balance, my knapsack catapulting into the darkness.

When I regained my perch and looked again, they had both disappeared. I scanned the dock, the path, the house. I even checked the bushes, but Jake and the dancer had totally vanished.

Trembling, I descended the tree, the bark grazing my arms. The sap oozed between my fingers and toes. I swung from one branch to the other, preoccupied by thoughts of how I might kill my boyfriend. In that one distracted moment, I forgot the springy branch. As my full weight landed on the limb, it ripped away from the trunk, sending me crashing downwards. I seemed to plunge in slow motion. I grabbed onto another branch and, for a split second, it held. Then I heard it snap. That's when I started to scream.

It seemed like an eternity that I lay frozen at the base of the tree, my face covered in loam and pine needles. I couldn't move, and was barely able to breathe. My head was spinning and I prayed for the dizziness to stop. Finally, I spit out a mouthful of dirt and slowly sat up. It was then that I felt something wet run down my cheek. My temples throbbed and I couldn't see. Was I blind, or was it just dark? My body hurt all over.

Slowly things started coming into focus and I made a valiant effort to struggle to my feet. Despite the pain, I found I could still walk. I combed the forest floor for my gear, but finally gave up looking for my shoes and precious pen. Anyhow, my hands and feet were black with dirt and tree sap. Hobbling out of the woods, I made my way slowly back to the car.

Four

When I limped into the emergency room, Kim was chatting at the desk with a doctor. She took one look at me and grabbed my arm. "What in God's green earth happened to you?"

With nothing in the car to stop the profuse bleeding, I had used my halter top to bind my head, digging out a yellowed Hudson's Bay coat from the hatch to replace my shirt. I must have looked like an apparition. The stares from the crowded waiting room confirmed this, followed by glares as Kim yanked me past them into the examination area. Some compensation for being best friends with an emergency room nurse.

She sat me down on a chair and untied the shirt. "Were you in a car accident?"

I shook my head.

She examined the cut on my forehead. "This is going to need a lot of stitches."

I looked down at my capris, splattered with blood.

"It has to be thirty degrees out. Why are you wearing this old winter jacket?" Kim sputtered. Unbuttoning it, she saw my bare chest underneath and laughed. She quickly threw me a hospital gown. "Let's get you cleaned up and get some paperwork done so I can get a doctor in here."

After twenty sutures, the doctor taped a thick bandage across my forehead. Kim handed me soap and a brush to scrub the blood and sap off my hands and arms. Avoiding the mirror, I scoured my fingers for ten minutes. The pine gum simply refused to come off. I then snuck a glance at my reflection. My cheeks were streaked with scratches and the skin around my left eye was beginning to swell. I shuddered. I had yet to tell Kim where I'd been or what I'd seen.

I peeked out from the cubicle. Looking official in her old-fashioned white nurse's uniform, Kim was helping an elderly woman onto a bed. I always teased her by calling her *Nurse Ratched*. She smiled at the next patient, her lipstick red against her white teeth. Even though the wait in the emergency room was hopelessly long, people would always ask for her by name.

"What the...." uttered Marlin, pulling open the curtain from the other side. For once he was speechless.

Kim handed him the prescription from the doctor. "She's in shock. I have no idea what happened except she keeps muttering something about a tree."

Five

In that one evening, my whole world turned inside out. The day after the stag, I successfully dodged leaving the house. Sensing my distress, Ziska became my constant companion. She followed my every move, snuggling up next to me on the chair, scrutinizing me with her large brown eyes.

I don't know which was worse, my black and blue face or the gossip about Jake and the stripper. My brother returned home from the coffee shop with a gift — a giant raspberry muffin. He announced that my boyfriend had yet to surface. The rumour mongers from the donut club were convinced he had run off with the dancer.

I envisioned the whole town lined up on Manitoba Street, pointing at me. "There! That's the girl whose almost-fiancé ran off with the stripper — you know, the stripper at the bachelor party that shot out of a cake, whipped cream flying everywhere." Not that there was any cream involved. My brother had constructed the cake from plywood — ironically, I had painted on the icing.

After giving me the cold shoulder for a day, Kim banged on the door. She had found out about my little party prank and the ensuing consequences. Standing on the threshold of the door, hands on her hips, she glared at me. She opened her mouth to speak, then turned, slamming the door behind her. A minute later she was back, flinging open the front door and yelling: "What were you thinking?"

"How was I supposed to know this could happen? You should have seen Boyd's face." I smiled, and then quickly frowned, moaning as one of the scabs on my face cracked open. I mumbled, "I thought it would make a great column."

"Where was this harlot from?" she retorted.

"What does that matter?" I sniffled, my nose running. Allergies, I was sure, from getting sap all over my hands and fingernails. I dragged myself off the couch.

She followed me into the bedroom. "It's important."

"John said she was from Hamilton." I plopped down on the bed.

Kim shook a finger at me. "I knew it. Real lowlifes live in Steel City."

I flung a pillow at her head. "Now there's a generalization if I've ever heard one. I'm sure that Hamilton is a normal city loaded with lots of everyday people. And besides, to follow your logic, doesn't it make everyone in Bracebridge a redneck?"

She nodded. "Right."

"You're a redneck?"

"Yes, but only a minor redneck," she quipped.

She then proceeded to recite story after story to prove her point. I laughed. I knew what she was up to: diverting my attention from my tragic circumstances. My small-town boyfriend had run off with a dancer from out of town and I was the laughing-stock of Bracebridge. It felt like I was in third grade all over again—compromised. Should I pick up that dog collar or leave it on the classroom floor? The nickname of *Unlucky* had taken me a decade to live down.

Kim flopped down beside me on my unmade bed. We lay in silence, side by side. Then she pulled on my pyjama leg. "Lying about in misery won't help. Get dressed, and we'll get sozzled."

I groaned. "Now that's a redneck suggestion if I've ever heard one. Shall we wander into the woods and look for our still?"

She rolled off the bed. "What a great idea. Let's go on a hike. A natural high." She opened the dresser, and tossed a pair of jeans at my head. "You've got five minutes to get ready."

The phone rang and I waved my hands at my brother through the open bedroom door. "If it's for me, I'm not home." But it was my boss and he insisted on speaking with me. I had called in sick, leaving a message on his voicemail. Mr. Sherman pulled no punches; he wanted me to write a personal interest story about the bachelor party. He called it my big break. What? This was the same man who had insisted controversial columns were off the table. That we worked for a small town daily, not *The Washington Post*. Previously, when I had tracked down a juicy story, I was told to cease and desist. The gall of the man! "It's simply too private," I gasped on the phone. "I can't do it." But he demanded that I come to the office at once.

I told Kim I'd meet her in half an hour outside my office. I quickly put on one of Marlin's baseball caps to hide the bandage, wore a long-sleeved shirt to cover my arms, and headed off, averting sidewalk stares.

Even on a normal day, my boss was particularly unattractive. His clothes hung on his frame, his eyes were set in deep sockets and his ears hung almost perpendicular to his head. My co-workers called him The Stiff. Despite his physical weaknesses, the man possessed an ego the size of the Hindenburg. I could never impress him with my double-triple fact checking and pristine notes. He didn't allow for discussion. He leaned forward in his oversized black leather office chair, hovering as I perched on the spindly guest chair opposite him. I felt his beady eyes on me. I was a mouse stuck in an open field and he was a hawk circling.

He swung his feet up on his desk, hands clasped behind his neck. "First, take off that hat and get Bert to snap some photos of your face. Then I want the full story. Find out where the guy and the girl took off to and get an interview. You know the routine." He slowly grinned at me. "What did the stripper hit you with? A baseball bat?"

A vein pulsated in my head. My jaw tightened. And then I snapped. I leapt to my feet and in one epic move swept his desk clean. Papers went soaring, coffee splattered and the electric pencil sharpener exploded against the wall, sending shavings flying everywhere. I ran out of the office, slamming the door behind me.

Six

Kim was waiting outside as planned. The last thing I felt like doing was going for a hike, but I felt obligated to join her.

It was at times like this that I really missed my mother. Her death had left our family in limbo. When I was sixteen, she had died of a brain aneurysm. People had said: "Isn't it lucky she didn't suffer a long-drawn-out disease like breast cancer?" Lucky? How was it lucky I didn't get to say goodbye? Especially since that particular morning I'd had a fight with her. She wouldn't let me go camping alone with Jake. I'd been fuming and called her a prude, which was actually absurd. She wasn't the least bit priggish. I'd only said it for shock value.

When I'm sleepless late at night, I go over our last conversation and try to fix it. No matter how I edit the scene, again and again, there is no way to go back. There is no compensation for losing your mother. Whether you're one or ninety-one. And especially if you haven't even graduated from high school yet.

It happened at the check-out counter at the IGA. Apparently, the grocery clerk had just told my mother she owed $72.61. A customer standing in line behind her saw her keel over and managed to grab her head before it struck the floor.

But she was already unconscious. I was called out of third period algebra class and told the news. I have hated math ever since.

As for my dad, he has never been the same. My parents had always fought like the movie critic team, Siskel and Ebert, seldom agreeing. Dad had been born in Athens, and my mother's family emigrated from a town outside of Dublin. Both had a propensity to be mulish, but they had a deep connection too. Even as a kid I understood it. His admiring glances. Her hands rubbing his shoulders after a long day at the restaurant. Their secret kisses when they thought no one was looking.

My mother was my hero. She was the best. Quirky. Fun. She made up wonderful stories and games and instilled in Marlin and me a hard-core devotion to reading. She was an accomplished seamstress, too. I remember her creating the world's most amazing costumes for Halloween. A witch or a clown costume was definitely verboten. The more outlandish the outfit the better. If you wanted to be a baked potato, she'd whip out the papier-mâché and construction paper. She'd stuff it with paper green onions and pink sponge bacon bits. She also staged the most unpredictable birthday events, almost never on the actual date. You'd wake up one morning and there would be a birthday cake instead of Shreddies and a pile of gifts wrapped in the comics from the Saturday paper. I got new pens, notebooks, and novels like *To Kill a Mockingbird*. One year, she gave me this thick pen that you could click and retract, selecting twenty-five different coloured inks.

Her laugh was contagious. It was impossible not to join in. The most boring of sitcoms suddenly became side-splitting. If she volunteered at a school event, every child in the class clamoured to sit next to her. She was my ace-in-the-hole. And heaven knows I needed that advantage. No one dared call me *Unlucky* on the days she visited.

It was actually my mother who helped me get through Kim's wedding. I didn't have far to go for an audience. She resided in a cherrywood box on the top shelf of the linen closet. After the funeral, Dad had placed her ashes in the living room. But the constant reminder was too agonizing. The three of us decided she would be better in the cupboard surrounded by her favourite Irish tablecloths.

On the afternoon following my tree fiasco, when Marlin and Dad left the house, I extracted Mom from the linens and set her on the coffee table. Ziska bounded up on the couch to watch. I put on the kettle and made a cup of tea—Mom liked Barry's Teas. We had a talk. Ziska joined in by eating the cookies. Gingerly, I broached the subject of my current dilemma. Mom told me I had absolutely no choice but to attend Kim's wedding. I couldn't walk out on my very best friend's nuptials. Her advice? If someone mentions Jake, become as deaf as a tree stump. She added that I'd be far too busy performing maid-of-honour duties to linger long in any one conversation. I finished my tea peacefully and placed her carefully back in the cupboard, resolving bravely to attend.

Seven

The morning of the wedding, Kim and I trundled off to her hairdresser, who cleverly disguised my injuries. First, she removed the lumpy white bandage and then used flesh-coloured Band-Aids to cover the stitches. She gently applied foundation over the yellow bruising. Finally, she swept my hair across my forehead. She must have used at least a thousand hair pins to conceal the wound. Thankfully, I was the only attendant, so there were no bridesmaids buzzing about asking questions.

For her wedding, Kim had designed her own calf-length dress. With her hair in a French twist and string of pearls around her neck, she looked like Grace Kelly ready for a movie set. She had also sewn my outfit. It was a cream-coloured blouse with a flowing sapphire-blue skirt. It showed off my tight waist but hid my thighs. Ideal for my pear-shaped body.

We finished dressing in her parents' bedroom. After primping, we reclined on her mother's lounge and toasted with a shot of ouzo. Opa! It was the end of an era for us. She would soon be a married and I had lost my one and only boyfriend. Nothing would ever be the same. We both admitted to feeling a little edgy.

As I walked down the aisle, I concentrated on Boyd's jubilant look of expectation. I didn't stumble once. Jake had been asked to be an usher, but much to my relief, he hadn't shown up. I felt skittish in the reception line but people seemed to brush past me, eager to greet the bride and groom. The best man and I made time pass by shaking hands and mumbling sweet nothings.

Suddenly the pilgrimage stopped dead. "Where's your boyfriend?" asked a piercing voice. I turned to see one of the MacKenzie sisters. I hadn't seen these girls in years. Rumour had it they'd disappeared into the big city after high school.

Coming to my rescue, John gushed as he took her hand, "Well, aren't you lovely tonight."

My childhood nemesis giggled. It was just enough to distract her. As she slipped away to congratulate Kim, John winked. He then excused himself to get us each a ginger ale. Upon his return, I took a big sip and almost choked. It was eighty percent rye. The bugger.

Later that evening, as I helped Kim change into her honeymoon outfit, she grabbed me by the shoulders and locked her eyes onto mine. "Why are you staying in Bracebridge?"

I shrugged my shoulders.

"Stop beating yourself up," she said. "Jake left a week ago without a word. Besides, you've known all along you couldn't stay here, not if you're serious about writing. This is your ticket, kiddo."

I mulled over her advice. Leave Bracebridge?

Kim then turned, asking me to undo her zipper. "What about Toronto? I've always wanted a place to crash there."

I reached over and hugged her. She pulled on her jeans and a t-shirt that read: *Nurses do it bedder*.

Part Two

Coming of Age

Eight

Reluctantly, I picked up a box from the tailgate of the truck. I dreaded lugging it up four flights of stairs to my new apartment. The hair at the back of my neck was already wet. Did I really need my entire collection of books? It goes without saying my father would have happily stored them at his house.

This was my first move and it brought back memories. For twenty-three years, I had lived on the old Bracebridge drive-in property. My father had bought it for a steal when he and Mom first arrived in town as newlyweds. They had renovated the snack bar into an odd-shaped, three-bedroom bungalow and the hulking movie screen and parking lot had become our playground. Since we lived on the edge of town, Marlin was my only playmate. He and I spent hours pretending the old speakers dangling from the leaning posts were radios to the Milky Way. Our imaginations were in constant overdrive. One day, we attempted to dig our way to China. We hit the water table and ended up with a mud pond. Another day, we built a spaceship out of old milk crates from the Bracebridge Dairy. When my dad decided to grow a vegetable garden, we pretended to be mountain climbers scaling Mount Everest.

My father had laboured on a Mediterranean ship before immigrating to Canada. It was only natural that he would transfer the nautical theme to our refurbished shack. He installed portholes in the bedrooms. Walls were painted stark white and doors were ocean blue like the Greek flag. The galley kitchen was only big enough for one person at a time. Pots and utensils hung overhead. The living room was our multipurpose area, serving as anything from our dining room to a workshop.

My chore each dinnertime was to unhook the wooden chairs from above the table. There wasn't much room to pull out the table out so my parents sat at either end, with my brother and me bumping elbows on the side. We did our homework there too. Our bedrooms were so cramped; I called mine my cell. Each included a twin bed, a small dresser and a wooden stool for a bedside table. At one point my dad had wanted to install hammocks, but thankfully, my mother vetoed that idea.

I still laugh recalling the Christmas our distant relatives drove up from New York State to visit. My brother and I were on the floor playing with my brand-new Etch-a-Sketch while the adults sipped cocktails. When mother asked me to set the table, my dad took it as his signal. He placed his Bloody Caesar on top of the television and flung open the front door. Without warning, he pitched the Christmas tree, decorations and all, into the snowbank. To us, it was part of the holiday tradition; it was a given we'd need extra room for the table. The expression on my great-aunt's face said it all. They never returned.

Marlin overtook me on the apartment staircase, carefully balancing a huge box. His swearing jarred me back to the present. As the unloading proceeded, his complaints became curses, then mutterings, and finally silence. Complaining was a waste of his energy. We were only halfway through unloading the truck.

"Why didn't you ask if the building had an elevator?" he sputtered. "Where are all your alleged friends?"

I shrugged my shoulders. "Kim would have helped, but I could hardly ask her to return from her honeymoon."

Dad had also offered, but that meant closing the restaurant for the day. "Don't worry," I told him. "It will be a simple process to move a few sticks of furniture and some boxes."

A foul odour lurked in the sauna-like stairwell. The outside temperature was over thirty-two degrees Celsius. I leaned against the wall on the second floor. My brother cruised past, sneering. He was anxious to get home, undoubtedly not wanting to miss a Saturday night with his pals.

"Get a move on, Pen," he said through clenched teeth.

I forced my feet to move, limping up the last steps and through the propped-open door, dropping my box with a thud.

"Maybe we could knock on a few doors and see if one of the neighbours will give us a hand?" said Marlin, as he plunked his load on the kitchen counter.

"Are you cracked?" I asked, wiping my brow. "This is Toronto, not Muskoka."

"Why did you pick this heap to live in, anyway?" he said.

"It was cheap and…" I said, rubbing my neck. "Anyhow, I have my trusty guard dog." Ziska was safely in her crate in the kitchen. We should have named her Underfoot.

The apartment contained four units on each level. The interior of the building was as bland as the outside; the corridor walls painted a murky beige, bumpy with hundreds of layers of paint. The hall floor was covered with mottled gray linoleum. I sniffed. There was that smell again—a stench of cooked cauliflower with an outhouse finish. I didn't remember the hallways reeking the day I applied for the vacancy. But then, I'd been sidetracked by the prospect of my own apartment on the top floor. Somehow, I'd missed the fact that the windows overlooked an alley of lean-to garages and overflowing garbage bins. It was hardly a penthouse view. It had also not crossed my mind that escorting Ziska up and down four flights of stairs to do her business might wear thin after a while.

Marlin rolled his eyes. I stuck out my tongue at him. What did he know about city life? For that matter, what did I know, either? I could count on one hand the number of times I had visited Toronto. He knocked on the door across from my apartment. I started to panic. Then it occurred to me. Who else would choose to live in such a building? "Don't," I said, fully expecting pale-skinned gypsies to emerge. I begged, "Marlin, stop!"

"Hello," he said loudly. "Anybody home?"

Ziska started to bark. No one answered. Marlin tried the next door. Then he placed his ear upon the wooden surface. "Someone's in there," he said, putting his eye up to the peep hole. "I can hear them." He banged again, harder. But no one opened the door. Just as he raised his hand to rap on the last door, an arm carrying a stool and a lamp appeared at the top of the stairs. Startled, I retreated inside the apartment.

A male voice asked, "Is this yours?"

"My sister's stuff," answered Marlin.

"The super told me a new tenant was moving in today. Since I was on my way up, I thought I'd lend a hand. Looks like there's tons left. Need help?"

The man's voice sounded pleasant. He was obviously a neighbour, so I realized I'd have to meet him eventually. Wiping my face with my shirttail, I stepped into the hallway. Without looking up, I replied: "Does a bear shit in the woods?"

I felt him turn in my direction. I was fixated on his fuzzy legs emerging from black bicycle shorts. Slowly raising my eyes, I saw this ginormous guy with a bushy beard, shaggy shoulder-length hair and the hairiest hands and arms I had ever laid eyes on. He started grinning.

"May I introduce myself," he said, holding out a hand. "I'm Bear."

I shook it. "My name is Paw…I mean Pen," I stuttered, my cheeks reddening. "And this is my brother, Marlin." My brother was tempted to burst out laughing, but was afraid he might get punched in the head.

"If we pull the lead out," said the guy, "we can get this done in two shakes of lamb's tail."

Despite the humidity and his bear-like hair, he had unending energy. Within half an hour, the truck was emptied. Boxes and furniture were piled high inside the living room. Thankfully, I'd had the foresight to plug in the fridge and chill some beer.

"We'd still be hauling stuff up if you hadn't come along," said my brother, pulling three icy bottles from the 1950s-style appliance. (That should have been a clue. The next day everything in the fridge was frozen solid.)

I gulped mine. It tasted wonderful.

"Where are you from?" Bear asked.

"Bracebridge," I answered. "It's a small…"

He interrupted. "Santa's Village, right?"

"Halfway to the north pole," said Marlin. "Hicksville." My brother liked to act like he was imprisoned in the outback. The fact is, he loved Muskoka and working as an apprentice to a local tradesman. I would have stayed too, except for Jake. I took another sip of beer and tried not to think about my ex. He hadn't even had the guts to send an email message. *BTW. We are over. I am alive and living with a stripper.* Period.

I opened Ziska's crate. She dashed to Bear's feet, wagging her bum.

"Is this one of those pot-bellied pigs?" asked Bear, picking her up and letting her chew on his beard.

"Not sure. We just know she's the boss," said Marlin. He was equally besotted with Ziska and had begged me to let her stay in Bracebridge.

"This is Ziska. She's a Bugg. Pug and Boston mix."

Bear sat on the arm of the couch, cradling the dog, letting her lick his hand. "So, what brings you here?"

I tore at the label on the bottle. "Looking for a job."

Marlin popped open another beer. "Good luck finding one when you don't even know your way around the city. She wouldn't recognize the corner of Yonge and Bloor if she tripped over it." I cleared my throat, and gestured to my brother to shut up. He pointed at me. "A school trip to the Metro Zoo doesn't count."

"Brothers!" I said, flinging a beer cap at his head. "When did you become such a bloody Toronto expert?"

Bear looked astonished. "You guys have never been downtown?"

I shook my head.

"Well, there's no time like the present!" He jumped to his feet and put down his half-empty bottle.

"What?" I said. "Now?"

"Let's blow this pop stand," he said.

Bear had an amusing penchant for clichés. To put it bluntly, he seemed rather strange. But the job of unpacking in this heat appeared overwhelming, especially since the apartment had no air conditioning. "I'm a bit sticky," I said, wiping my face on my shirttail again.

"Sally will take care of that," he said.

"Who?" asked Marlin.

"Take care of what?" I spoke up, grabbing my purse, keys, and Ziska. I bolted the door and trailed down three flights of stairs behind the guys.

To my brother's initial disappointment, Sally was not a girl. But when Bear opened the garage door, Marlin let out a long whistle. Inside appeared a sky-blue 1964 Oldsmobile in mint condition. Bear reversed the car into the laneway and pushed a button. With a rumble, the roof lifted up and then down. My brother dove into the passenger seat, completely forgetting about me. Ziska jumped onto his lap. Bear opened his door and pulled the seat forward, and I squeezed into the back.

I had never ridden in a convertible. I felt like some kind of sweat-covered prom queen waving to onlookers as we puttered down the street. Bear hit the gas pedal and we drove up the ramp to the Gardiner Expressway. We barrelled down the highway, the wind whipping my hair into knots. As we turned and floated up Yonge Street, my heart was pounding. There were so many people lining the sidewalks. It looked like the world's greatest party. My brother had a huge grin on his face. He was resting his arm casually on the passenger door as if this joy ride was a weekend ritual. Ziska stood on his lap, ears back, nose to the breeze and tongue hanging out.

Tapping Marlin on the shoulder, I chimed in, "Nothing like Manitoba Street, eh?" — Bracebridge's main drag.

As he drove, Bear chatted about local history, showing us different neighbourhoods — Little Italy, Rosedale, The Annex, Chinatown and Kensington Market. It was tough wrapping my mind around the size of Toronto. He switched stations on the radio, and as he did, my favourite Gord Downie song, *Ahead by a Century*, floated through the car.

I felt my chest constrict, my tongue go dry. The Tragically Hip. Our favourite band. Jake and me. Except not anymore. Not our anything. I put my hands over my ears.

"Do you mind if I change the station?" my brother asked. Without turning his head, he could sense my reaction.

Our excursion seemed to be ending at the bottom of the Leslie Street spit. "So, what do you think of Hogtown?" our tour guide asked.

I leaned over the seat. "It's huge, but for some reason it doesn't seem so daunting now."

"We're only a few minutes from the apartment and it's close to six. Do you want to put on the feedbag?" he asked.

"Yeah, I could eat the asshole out of a skunk," said Marlin, adding a Muskoka colloquialism into the mix.

They both snorted. "Good one, Fish," said Bear.

Marlin turned to poke me. "You owe me a major feast, dear sister."

I tapped Bear on the shoulder. "Are you sure we're not holding you up from something?"

He ignored the question. "Do you like Greek?"

Marlin and I looked at each other and grinned.

It was then I decided the city wasn't as cold as everyone had said. With our plates piled high with pork souvlaki, rice, roast potatoes and salad, it was like coming home. Bear talked non-stop about his job and his fiancée. Dipping a chunk of meat into the Tzatziki sauce, I sighed with relief. He had a girlfriend. That meant we could just be friends and avoid the sexual overtones. Not that I was attracted to him. Eye candy he was not!

We dined on a patio, the dog at our feet. I noticed Bear sneak pieces of meat to Ziska. I quietly reflected. It was auspicious to find a friend on the first day. And he was funny, too. I could use a few laughs.

Nine

If my neighbour resembled a bear, his girlfriend looked like a giraffe. Exotic Giselle. It appeared as if she applied her eye makeup from a vat of mascara and a caulking gun of eyeliner. She refused to call me by my nickname, but pronounced my name Pen-L-O-Pee. As she emphasized the *Pee*, she would glare down at me with disdain. Each time my stomach rolled. No question about it, she was triggering me big time.

Later that week, I met Bear's roommate, Lucas. I couldn't stop gawking. Could there be life after Jake? I shoved aside ex-boyfriend thoughts just enough to concentrate on my new neighbour. He made cutting toenails erotic. Shirtless, jeans slung low on his hips, he leaned over the coffee table clipping his nails, collecting them in an ashtray. He was intense in his labour. He stopped for a second, and tucked a lock of blonde hair behind his ear.

Bear had invited me in for cocktails — Brown Cow night. As I sat in the kitchen sipping the ice-cold Kahlua and milk, I kept one eye on his roommate in the other room.

"Pen?" asked Bear.

"What?"

"You didn't answer my question."

I put my glass down on the turquoise Formica table. "Excuse me?"

"How did your first week go?"

"Not good." I didn't have the energy to describe my horrific week.

Bear cleared his throat. "Not good in what way? What happened?"

"Maybe later," I uttered.

To start with, the telephone company had lost my order. The phone was scheduled to be hooked up Monday, but still hadn't been installed. Their customer service told me to make sure I was at the apartment between eight and five. Every day I had waited dutifully with anticipation, but nobody showed up. Then on Thursday, while talking to company rep number 436, I was told they had no record of my request. In desperation I bought a cell phone. It was a luxury I could scarcely afford. But how can you job hunt without a phone? I picked the pay-as-you-go plan — the cheapest. I raced home to the apartment. After allowing the battery to fully charge, I flipped it open and pushed the on button. The tiny screen lit up for two and a half seconds, then blinked off. The thing was a lemon and had to be returned.

As for my first week on the job front, I was under some naive illusion I could just walk into a city newspaper and get a job. I started with a visit to *The Globe and Mail*. The receptionist narrowed her eyes at me when I explained my phone situation. As if not wanting to touch my paperwork, the woman used claw-like nails to accept my resume. She slid it behind the counter, hit a purifying cream pump on the counter five times and answered the next call. I'm positive my resume landed in the recycling bin.

Bear clinked his glass against mine. "C'mon. Fess up."

Fortunately, Giselle loped through the apartment door and I was saved. "Don't you boys ever clean up?" she whined. Upon seeing me, she sneered, her long neck arching, her lip curling as if she had lettuce stuck in her front teeth. I used that moment to escape.

Ten

Closing my front door, I felt a lump building in my throat. Why did I rashly move here, knowing no one, having no job? I switched on the light and studied my living room. A list was tacked to the bulletin board over my timeworn desk.

1. Unpack
2. Clean apartment
3. Get phone installed
4. Print resumes
5. Get a job

Two out of three. Last week had been filled with unpacking and rearranging my odd assortment of hand-me-down furniture. My Aunt Binkie from Staynor had bought a new couch and offered me her old one; it was teal blue spattered with geometric lime-green shapes. Not exactly my taste, but was in near-new condition. It would come to be known as "the eyesore." On the upside, my dad surrendered a tattered but cherished wing chair. He also bought me a double mattress as my first apartment gift. My kitchen was three times larger than our galley at home. At a second-hand store in Orillia, I'd found a bargain. For thirty-two bucks, I scored a café table and two matching caned chairs. But my prized possession was in the living room—bookshelves—an inheritance from my mother.

The first poster I tacked to the wall was a list of Murphy's Laws. *If anything can go wrong, it will.* Other twenty-something-year-old females might have had photos of mischievous kittens or a head shot of Heath Ledger. I was a tad less optimistic.

After I dragged the empty cartons down to a bin in the alley, my apartment looked bare. Since I had tons of time on my hands — you can't job hunt without a phone — I started scouring the apartment. It took me a whole day to wash the windows, carrying each frame into the bathtub to rinse off decade-thick layers of sludge. I must have had blinders on when I viewed the apartment. Perhaps I had been mesmerized by the enormous size of the bedroom after a lifetime of living in a closet. I'd certainly overlooked the state of the bathroom. No amount of scrubbing could bring back the tub enamel, and the floor tiles remained grey despite the jug of bleach I dumped on them. As I zealously attacked the faucets, my thoughts drifted back to my old life in Bracebridge.

I hadn't thought it through. Here I was in Toronto. No friends, no family, no money for cable television. I'd already watched my favourite DVDs at least once. I was alone again on a Saturday night, but in a city far, far away. I heard someone laughing in the hallway and felt tears starting to well up. Sitting on the braided rug in front of my bookcase, I raised the bevelled glass door and selected a book. Opening up the cover, I read: *To Pen, Love Jake*. I hurled the book across the room, splitting its spine. Ziska chased after it, grabbing it in her teeth, shaking it like prey. I felt my anxiety starting to build. I shoved my feet into my sandals, grabbed my keys, Ziska and her leash, and headed out the door. I needed air. I needed to clear my brain.

Eleven

Bear proved to be a good neighbour. Later that same week, he asked me back to his apartment. We were alone; Giselle was visiting her sister and Lucas had left for the cyber cafe to write poetry. I lounged on a beanbag chair and Bear sat on the futon, guitar under his arm. Ziska propped her head on his knee. Like mine, their apartment was filled with castoffs. A bulky television sat on a board placed across two stacks of bricks. In one corner there was a three-foot carved heron wearing a baker's hat. In the other was a floor to ceiling rack of CDs.

Bear picked up his guitar and began to strum. "Here's one you might know," he said. "Big, bad bear," he sang. "Oh, how big. Oh, how bad." He sounded like a cow that was days past milking. I covered my ears. He stopped his impromptu ballad and started to sing the Tragically Hip's song, *Wheat Kings*. To hell with Jake. I loved that song. Joining the chorus, I begged for more. Bear could obviously sing anything from Johnny Cash to Green Day. I watched his fingers plucking the strings and wished I could carry a tune.

After the impromptu music recital, he prepared a tray of nachos, burying them in green onions, jalapenos, tomatoes and a mountain of grated cheddar. He handed me an icy mug of beer. Tonight it was Steam Whistle Pilsner night.

"Tell me," I asked, "what's your real name?"

"Ted." He cleared a spot for the platter on the coffee table.

I smiled. "Teddy?"

He sipped his beer. "Yup."

"Really? As in Teddy Bear?" I sat on the floor cross-legged. Ziska sat beside me, nose twitching—not exactly begging, but ever hopeful that someone would drop a gob of cheese or a chip.

"How do you think I got the nickname Bear?" he answered with a poker face.

I looked dubious.

He cracked a smile. "I'm kidding. It's really Edward." I punched him in the arm, hard. "OK, OK, I confess," he said, leaning away. "My true name is Winnifred."

"And mine is Desire," I said, shaking my head.

He laughed. "Okay, okay. I'll tell you the actual name on my birth certificate. But you must swear never to disclose it. Not to anyone. Ever." He looked furtively around the living room as if someone might be hiding behind the wooden bird. "I'm Pennington E. Worthington... the Third."

My upper lip curled. "You think you can carry this on forever?"

"Slice of toast," he said, smirking. I knew what he meant: piece of cake. I had caught on to his code.

After a difficult initial few days, spending time with my new neighbour was easing my transition from country to city girl. It turned out Bear was also a master baker. Despite the fact he worked for a conglomerate bakery whose claim to fame was rock-hard ginger cookies, his specialty was miniature butter tarts. He convinced me he didn't have to eat baked goods. By handling the ingredients, the sweet calories just soaked into his skin. "Here's the baker's dozen," he said, jiggling his belly.

"I need a new career," he then added, tossing a packet of matches onto my lap. It read: *You too can be a radio operator, welder, electrical technician, office administrator or medical secretary.* "Giselle wants me to become a professional." The woman worked at a recycling plant, not exactly a glamorous vocation and certainly at odds with her ambitions for him. As if reading my thoughts, he explained that she modelled part-time, and handed me a portfolio. Most of the glossy photos were of Giselle's neck, clad in what appeared to be diamond necklaces.

I handed him back the matches and changed the subject. "I like tarts," I said. "Will you make me some?"

His eyes lit up. "How many dozens?"

I thought about my other new acquaintance, Lucas, and how I had met him one afternoon on the stairs. He was dressed in a Canadian Tire uniform and had a hefty thesaurus tucked under his arm. He looked at me in bewilderment. Then a light must have gone on and he nodded, asking, "Any luck, Pet?" Even in this ill-fitting outfit Lucas looked tasty, but I was not about to bounce into a new relationship.

I reminded myself about the list I had made:

1. Men are deceitful.
2. The opposite sex is selfish and self-serving.
3. Men are narcissistic.
4. Males are generally infuriating.
5. Whatever you do, no rebound relationships.

Twelve

During the second week of job hunting I woke up to find that the city had disappeared under a cloud of smog. The air was clammy as I trudged to the subway, a stack of resumes in my backpack. I could scarcely see the next crack in the sidewalk. Breathing carefully through my mouth, I tried to avoid the sewer gas smell that hung in the atmosphere. Thoughts of Muskoka's sweet air with the aroma of pine needles came to mind. Then it occurred to me. If I didn't find a job soon I might have to crawl back to that fresh air. My money was running out. The first and last month's rent had put a punishing dent in my savings.

Despite the smell, I was beginning to like the-nobody-makes-eye-contact urban lifestyle. I hadn't met anyone else, other than the three from next door. And they had no inkling of my past. A revelation came to mind. Why not re-invent myself? Cut my hair, spruce myself up. Run up my credit card with some new clothes, and get makeup instructions at *The Bay* cosmetics counter. Why not? Just do everything the opposite. No more kowtowing to anyone. I'd demand a job. Start asking men out. I glanced down. My hands were clenched in fists — my feet were spread wide in a fighting stance.

I realized I must have looked funny standing there like a statue in the fog. I marched down the street and found the nearest hair salon. Before I lost my nerve, I commanded, "Chop it all off." I shut my eyes while the scissors snipped. I kept them closed as the blow dryer whipped my fine hair.

"Done," said the stylist.

I opened one eye. A stranger stared back at me.

"This is a much better cut for your face," said the hairdresser.

As I turned my head from side to side, I noticed it felt eleven times lighter. The cut was short, parted on the side with bangs swooping over one eye. I almost looked cute.

I strutted back to the subway entrance feeling ready to take on the world. Then I abruptly stopped at the stairs. What was next on my new agenda? Bumping into me, a man muttered under his breath. I moved out of the way and in that moment, decided my quest for a new career could start on Monday. One step at a time.

As I reached the third landing of my building I heard a phone ringing in the distance. It wasn't until I shoved the key into the door lock that I realized it was mine. I had plugged my new portable phone into the jack left by the old tenants. For a few seconds, I stared at it, hesitating. But then it rang one more time, and I grabbed the receiver.

"Hey, Pen," said a familiar voice. "Want some company?"

Thirteen

"When did you get back from your honeymoon?" I asked.

"Yesterday," said Kim, a note of mirth in her tone. "We came home a few days early because my new husband had an argument with some poison ivy."

"Where did you go?" Boyd had insisted on keeping the honeymoon destination a secret.

"On a bicycle tour of the Cabot Trail," she replied. "It was amazing. You have to go. We camped on these cliffs overhanging the ocean and ate tons of potato bread and lobster. But during our second week, Boyd walked off the trail to do a little business and sat in a patch. Before he figured out what it was, he scratched his leg, then touched his face and arms. The man is one big angry rash."

"Poor guy," I said. Just thinking about it made me want to scratch.

She sighed. "Yeah, he's a mess. Give me the directions to your place. My bag is packed and I'm coming to The Big Smoke."

"You're leaving him to suffer alone?"

"His mommy is right upstairs," she said. "He actually told me to go away. It seems I'm coddling him and he needs a day or two to himself." Kim and Boyd were temporarily renting a basement apartment from his parents.

Kim arrived three hours later and started looking for an overnight parking spot. Having no idea about visitor parking, I knocked on Bear's door. He was unloading a liquor store box in the kitchen and motioned us in.

"Good, you're just in time to try my new invention. It came to me just this morning. A daiqarita. It's a cross between a daiquiri and margarita. Candy is dandy but liquor is quicker."

Kim pushed her way past me, and introduced herself. Many cocktails later, she let news of my recent relationship history slip. The alcohol had relaxed me, and I decided I didn't care that Bear knew about my disastrous love story. I heard the two conspiring, deciding that what I needed was a new boyfriend, especially with my snazzy new haircut. Listening to their plans, I began to feel woozy.

I leaned back on a cushion and shut my eyes but my ears perked up when I heard Kim mention that even Jake's mother hadn't heard from him. That was strange. He wasn't the most responsible person in the world, but it didn't seem right that he hadn't called home yet or officially quit his job. To disappear into the night was simply not like him. We all assumed he ran off with the girl. But what if this wasn't true? What if he was at the bottom of Lake Rosseau? Now I felt like a coward for not calling his mother before I left.

"Personally, I'm glad the guy took off," said Kim.

I popped open my eyes and sat up. "Why do you say that?"

She tilted her head. "I tried to tell you so many times. Jake didn't treat you well."

Before I could open my mouth, Bear leapt from his chair, spilling his glass. "Eureka! What about Lucas?" he said pulling a photo off the fridge for Kim.

"Who's he?" asked Kim, grinning and waving the picture like it was too hot to hold.

"My roommate. He's currently unattached, and he's a writer too. A poet," he replied, winking. "And I have an inkling our Pen has a crush on him."

"No, no." I stood up shakily, swooning and waving my hands. "Kim, we've gotta go!" I grabbed her arm. "We need to find you a parking spot, now!"

A loud banging woke us up the next morning. Ziska shot to the door, yowling. I told her to sit and be quiet. She obeyed for a second, but finding it was Bear, she jumped up to greet him. He was holding a picnic basket, insisting we dress lickety-split as he was escorting us on the ferry to the Toronto Islands. "Yes!" said Kim. "We'll be down in a flash."

When we met him in the alley, Lucas was sitting in the back seat of the car.

"You must be the in-house poet I've heard so much about," said Kim, extending her hand. En route to the terminal, she chattered non-stop, admiring the sights, telling Bear horror stories of her job in the ER, and to my embarrassment, asking Lucas to recite one of his poems.

"You wouldn't like my stuff," he mumbled. For the past fifteen minutes, he hadn't said more than three words. I sat beside him in the back seat, both of us looking out of opposite sides of the car, Ziska between us.

Kim twisted in her seat. "What kind of poetry do you write?"

Bear answered for him. "Dark, gory themes."

This piqued my interest. "Do you like Edward Gorey?"

My seatmate looked annoyed. "Who?"

"A is for Amy who fell down the stairs," said Bear, pulling into a parking lot under the expressway.

"B is for Basil assaulted by bears," I continued, almost choking with laughter before everyone joined in, except Lucas. He just frowned.

The ferry to Ward's Island wasted no time. By the time we zigzagged through the mob of people, strollers, dogs and bicycles to the front, the crew was already tying up at the island. The gate opened and we trailed onto the dock and down a gravel pathway.

The crowd dissipated to the right as Bear directed us into a clutch of narrow lanes between dollhouse-like cottages and tangled gardens. A mauve, two-storey house with pink trim had a rusted Johnson 10-horsepower motor clamped beside the gate. It was exactly the model my dad had on his old fishing boat. In another garden, geraniums were planted in a claw-foot tub and pansies in a chipped toilet. Yards were filled with trellises adorned with climbing clematis, gnomes and tiny stone patios. I gazed out across the water at Toronto. It felt surreal to be so far from Muskoka, walking among these whimsical homes yet so close to skyscrapers piercing the downtown sky.

Jake and I had rarely left Bracebridge except when we commuted to college. In the six years we'd been together, we had only visited his father in North Bay twice, and it was under duress. He despised his dad for leaving his mother. His parents were divorced when he was thirteen. He and his mother had moved to his grandparents' home in Bracebridge.

One summer I had convinced Jake to go to Stratford to see *A Midsummer Night's Dream*. But even then, he pressured me into returning that very same night. He was obsessive about missing a session at the fitness club. I had joined the club too, but after a few months found every excuse not to go and dropped my membership. It was tedious using those Stairmasters or spin bikes, and besides, I hated looking at myself in the floor-to-ceiling mirrors.

I thought about Kim's comment from the night before. I had been trying hard not to think about Jake. The very last thing he'd said to me was to stop eating Quality Street chocolates. I thought he was joking, but the expression on his face was one of disgust. He'd also nagged me to get a better-paying job, stating that journalism was simply not lucrative.

Bear was pointing out a house with seven skylights when we heard Lucas groan. He removed his sunglasses and wiped his forehead with the back of his hand. "When are we going to the beach?" He sounded like a petulant three-year old.

I grabbed Bear by the arm. "Let's get this party started!" Our tour guide led us down another row of houses and past a park with a ball diamond that ended up at a sandbar on the south end of the island. The men pulled off their shirts. One's chest was like a cashmere sweater and the other's was as smooth as a baby's bum. Kim's eyes grew wide. She winked at me and kicked off her sandals. It's all I heard about for the rest of her visit.

Fourteen

Later that week, I ran into Bear at a sidewalk café on the Danforth. I was eating Tahini cake and reading the Go Train schedule.

"Where are you off to?" he asked.

I looked up. "Hamilton."

"On a tour of the Stelco plant?" He sat down at my table.

"I'm looking for someone," I said, folding the paper.

He studied me, one eye shut. "The boyfriend?" He waved at the waiter for a coffee.

I didn't answer, pushing the map and schedule into my bag.

"None of my beeswax," he said, ripping open a sugar packet. "But if you want a ride, or need some help, you know where to find me."

"Thanks," I mumbled, realizing it might actually be good to have some company.

I knew the stripper's name, at least her stage name: Ginger Barton. I suspected there was probably an orange-coloured cat in her past. I'd searched on the internet for a Barton Street in Hamilton. Bingo. But it was several kilometres long, stretching from one side of the city to the other. I bought a map book and tucked it into my purse.

Bear showed up on the evening of our expedition wearing a Sherlock Holmes hat and a camouflage shirt. As we drove past Oakville, on the outskirts of Toronto, fat raindrops the size of quarters hit the windshield. He quickly swerved onto the shoulder and closed the roof of the convertible. Within minutes the sky turned black. We had the headlights on and the windshield wipers at full speed. The wind buffeted the car as we crossed the Skyway Bridge. Bear gripped the steering wheel, fighting to stay in his lane. I looked over the railing, staring into the dark water of the bay below. I scribbled a note into my book: *oil slick*.

As we drove down Burlington Street, a flash of lightning lit the sky, exposing a landscape of industrial buildings, devoid of greenery, surrounded by miles of chain-link fence. It was hard to imagine people working in those buildings. The road snaked by the gloomy superstructures. Overhead a pipe exploded with light, burning off gases. In the adjacent lane, a truck with a massive flatbed trailer trundled past us. I thought to myself: if that steel load accidentally rolled off, we'd be flattened like bugs. I stopped making notes and closed my eyes. In my mind, I imagined robots and non-stop cog wheels. Bear's car had transformed into a DeLorean. We were venturing through a space-age factory world.

As the downpour slowed, we crawled along Barton Street, passing empty, unlit storefronts with faded newspapers taped over windows. Only a cheque-cashing outlet with its yellow blinking sign was open. I couldn't help wondering: Did Jake leave Muskoka for this?

Our outing to Hamilton was a flop; Barton Street was mega blocks long. I must have been out of my head to believe we could just cruise the area and find Miss Ginger. I had searched the faces of pedestrians, seeing my ex-boyfriend everywhere. I even leapt out of the car at an intersection when I saw a blonde-haired man strutting down the sidewalk. Of course, it wasn't him.

No further ahead, we drove back to Toronto.

Fifteen

The library branch at Pape and Danforth soon became my second home. I used the photocopier to pump out resumes — at a dime a shot — as I pored through newspaper classifieds. One stormy morning while waiting for the rain to stop, I read the entire book *What Color is Your Parachute*. Was I really in the right vocation? I had hand-delivered and mailed a stack of resumes, but not one newspaper or magazine had called me for an interview.

I hadn't realized how out of touch I was. I read an article about how the big newspapers were laying off. The internet, blogs and other forms of electronic journalism were turning reporters into dinosaurs. Had I been in a time warp? I began applying to other postings, any job. I considered asking my dad for a loan but he wasn't flush with cash. The restaurant business had steadily declined since the big chains had arrived in town. People preferred to go to a drive-thru to pick up their burgers.

Bear told me he knew some people and he could probably get me work. He warned, however, that the jobs probably wouldn't pay much. I assured him that at this point I'd do anything. That's how I got my start in the men's clothing department of Honest Ed's. When I arrived for the interview, I thought I had entered an amusement park. The store's façade boasted a blinking red and yellow sign an entire block long. The manager bragged about how it required over twenty thousand bulbs to light it up.

The inside of the store was crammed with merchandise of every description, from hairspray to pizza trays, diapers to running shoes. Hand-painted signs were tacked up, advertising specials or directing you to an exit. Black and white photos of movie stars from the past lined the walls: Dean Martin, Ingrid Bergman and Marlene Dietrich. The building was an acre wide, with bins and shelves lit overhead by fluorescents that made everyone's face look blue. My head was spinning at the end of my first day.

Honest Ed's would be my rent money. But I planned to continue writing. I'd freelance on the side. My plan was to build my resume and experience by getting published. After a few days at the store, I soon realized that the job might actually be good fodder for a personal essay. I looked around at the shoppers. A woman in a babushka was sorting through a rack of men's sweatshirts. She caught my eye because she reminded me of Edith Prickley from SCTV. A man came up behind her and pinched her bum. I was going to call security, but she swatted his hand away and continued to look for a size. Then I realized… it was her husband.

I bought a new Moleskine notebook and started jotting down observations at work and especially on the subway, to and from work. Mostly I appraised women. One day, while riding the Red Rocket home, the lyrics from the old-time song, *I've Got a Lovely Bunch of Coconuts*, whizzed out of my lips. Startled, I stopped singing aloud and looked up. But no one was paying any attention to me. The train was full of wacky riders. As I watched the women on the train I noticed many wearing clothes either too tight or too large. Definitely worth recording.

1. Woman pulling the bottom of her shirt down. Obsessively.
2. Too tight high heels. Keeps slipping her foot out of shoe, bright pink line indenting her skin.
3. Woman in men's pyjama pants. Odd Christmas theme in summer?
4. See-through shirt. Bra straps digging into shoulder.
5. Disappearing skirt. When she stood up to exit train, practically a belt.
6. Biggest hoodie this side of the Rockies. Can't see her knees.
7. Short shorts. Lime green, nonetheless.
8. Jeans like leotards. Every roll revealed.
9. Tent dress. Caftan. How many women are hiding in there?
10. Tailored shirt. Two middle buttons popped off, almost taking my eye out.

I looked down at my own attire. Weren't my pants getting a little snug? I slammed my notebook shut, put my Micron 05 behind my ear and started reading the subway advertisements overhead.

Sixteen

The next morning, I woke up late. I slid open my closet door and caught a glimpse of myself in the mirror, wearing what I termed my "battleship" underwear; gray and big enough to sink the Titanic. Slowly I turned, twisting and examining my backside. It was more than huge. No wonder Jake ran for the hills. Quickly I hopped into my pants, breathing in deeply, tugging up the zipper. There seemed to be more bumps and bulges than usual and minimal breathing room. I vowed to start walking to work, or at least part way. Yes, and I would brown-bag lunch instead of munching on tire-size cinnamon buns. How many times had I studied diet plans, talked about calories and carbs and getting in shape? In the past, Jake had enthusiastically made me charts and set my goals. I'd promise myself that when I lost twenty pounds I'd buy sexy underwear. What the heck was I waiting for?

I wondered about the other women I'd been studying on the subway. Were they all in limbo too, praying for the good body fairy to arrive and wave her wand? I had been floundering, looking for a writing theme that struck a chord with me. Glaring at myself in the mirror, I realized I had found it—women and body image. I grabbed my notebook and a handful of pens, scribbling questions onto the page.

1. Do you like your figure?
2. If not, at what age did you start to criticize yourself?
3. Have you ever been on a diet? How many times have you been on a diet?
4. Did anything help?
5. Have you joined any weight-loss programs?
6. Have you ever read any self-help books?
7. Do you binge eat?

The phone rang. I picked up the receiver.

"Pen?"

I swallowed hard, recognizing the voice. It was Ann, Jake's mother.

"I'm sorry to bother you. I dropped into the restaurant and your father gave me your phone number." Her words sounded pinched. "Have you heard from Jake at all?"

"No," I replied. "Haven't you?"

Ann mumbled, "You have no idea at all where he could be?"

I played with the phone cord. "He hasn't been in touch with you?" This was a guy who never left Bracebridge, and up to a few weeks ago, had eaten his Weetabix every morning with his mama.

"Only the night he left," she said. "He called me to say he was leaving town for a while but he'd be in touch." I felt a surge of anger, the vision of his body drifting at the bottom of the lake vanishing. "I had no idea what was going on when he woke me up. I presumed he meant he was leaving with you, that you two were eloping. But then I heard all the talk in town."

I put the phone receiver to my chest. He'd never proposed and we'd never discussed the subject. I had sensed his reluctance, forever reeling from his parents' divorce. I was just happy to be with him, assuming one day he'd get over it and we'd marry. We shared a pizza every Friday night at Bill's, we attended my brother's hockey games, we drank wine with Kim and Boyd, and we had sex every Wednesday and Friday like clockwork. I had considered our relationship acceptable, but then, what did I have to compare it to? We were in a groove, I thought.

I put the phone back to my ear. "I don't know what to tell you. But he hasn't contacted me."

Ann blew her nose loudly. "I've heard more rumours running through Bracebridge and I thought you might have some clue. Was he acting peculiar before this whole incident?"

"No, business as usual." Why did I refer our relationship this way? Like it was some sort of company transaction. I pushed the thought away. "Look, Ann, I'm just as mystified as you. I was under the impression he and I were...."

She interrupted. "What about this dancer? Someone told me you hired her."

I really didn't feel like explaining myself. "It was a practical joke — I only suggested the notion of the cake. It was silly and..." I paused. Why was I blathering? "Someone else hired her."

"Who?" she demanded.

Should I tell her it was John? Or should I say I didn't know? Her son had left me. It wasn't my personal duty to locate him, my job to set this straight. "I'll find out for you."

She sighed. "Thanks, Pen, I know this has been a nightmare for you too but I've been sick with worry. I thought he would have called by now. I keep thinking maybe he hit his head, and is suffering from amnesia or..." Her voice drifted off. I assured her that since he did contact her before he left, he was probably fine—maybe some kind of mid-twenties crisis. I promised to call once I found out anything.

I grabbed my purse and keys, glanced at Bear's door and wondered if he was game for a trip to Gravenhurst. I felt bad for dragging Bear into this mess, but he told me it was more fun than a barrel full of Monchhichis.

As I turned to pull my apartment door shut behind me, I felt two hands shove me back inside. Giselle glanced around my living room with distaste. "Keep your hands off my boyfriend," she snarled. She was wearing a leopard-print miniskirt, a white and black striped halter top and gold hoop earrings the diameter of pie plates.

I laughed nervously. "What?"

"Lucas told me someone stole your boyfriend, but no one is taking my man," she hissed, stabbing me in the chest with her French manicured fingernail.

I was stunned; I was back into grade school again. I looked around for a weapon. "We're simply friends, end of story. I have no idea why you've barged in here like this, but let me set you straight. I do not want Bear. I will never want him. The Bear is yours!"

Hearing the kerfuffle, Bear burst into my apartment, just in time to see me wielding a toilet brush in his girlfriend's face. She swatted it away, and stomped out the door. He chuckled. "I've never had anyone duel over me before."

I was fuming. "What's her problem?"

He scratched his head. "Don't take her seriously. She's a drama queen and loves to make scenes. I told her about our Hamilton extravaganza and she flipped out."

"I guess a trip to a Gravenhurst strip club is out of the question then?"

He clapped his hands and gave me a high five. "I'm in like Flynn. When do you want to go?"

"Tomorrow, after work?"

Seventeen

This time Bear wore his man-about-town outfit. At least, that's what he called it. The back of his short-sleeved shirt sported a large image of a dog driving a convertible. His ensemble was topped off with a bowler hat. Not quite the undercover look I'd hoped for.

I thought a weeknight might be less crowded for inter-rogating the staff about Miss Barton. But when we arrived the parking lot was jammed. The club looked like a concrete bunker with a flashing neon sign overhead.

"You go. I'll wait for you at the car," I said, backing away from the door. "Be sure to ask one of the girls, not the manager. They might be more likely to give you information."

Bear pushed me forward. "Come on. You need a drink. Let's case the joint together and figure out our best candidate."

After my eyes adjusted to the lighting, I could see that the place was crammed with men, many still in work clothes. The sour odour of stale beer permeated the air. I almost stumbled when a nasal voice interrupted the music, booming from the loudspeaker, "She'll be right out!" Chair legs scraped the concrete floor as the patrons swung around to face the stage. Bear guided me through the crowd to a table in the far corner. When the audience started to whistle and hoot, I turned to see a frizzy-haired woman in a negligee run onto the stage. She began performing intimate acts to Def Leppard music, using a series of stuffed animals. I tried not to gawk, but the performer reminded me of the Gilda Radner character, Roseanne Roseannadanna, of ancient *Saturday Night Live* fame. The act scarcely seemed erotic. What could men possibly see in this?

As I perched on the stool, carefully avoiding the surface of our table, a gum-cracking waitress, wearing cut-off jean shorts and a revealing halter top, leaned down to wipe the sticky table top. Having no cleavage of my own, I was mesmerized by the crater between this woman's breasts.

After ordering two draft beers, Bear inquired if she knew any of the strippers. "Look, buster," she said, with one hand balancing a tray, "these girls dance — that's it. This is a gentleman's club, not a whorehouse." She was pushing it here.

Bear shook his head. "No, no, I didn't mean that." But the server had already stalked off, shouted to the barman and disappeared through a door. The bartender reefed on the beer tap, and motioned for us to come collect the glasses.

I waved my hand, signalling Bear to stay put. I strutted up to the bar, sliding onto a vacant stool. "Was there a girl called Ginger Barton working here this summer?" I asked, letting my hair fall into my face, and then flipping it back.

He nodded.

"Is she still around?"

He shook his head.

"Do you know where I can contact her?"

He shrugged his shoulders. My frustration grew. It was like talking to a Bobblehead doll. I could hardly concentrate with the noise behind me.

I yelled, "Do you know what her real name is?"

His response was lost in whistles and jeers. I could feel my face turning red. I couldn't wait to get out of this place. I put my notebook down in front of the barkeeper and handed him my pen. He scratched down a name. I thanked him, carrying the beer mugs to the table. I peered down at what he had written: *Mary Smith*. I groaned. With a name like that, we'd be searching for centuries. I guzzled the drink. Bear took one sip, grimaced and pushed it away.

I apologized as we walked back to the car. "I can't believe I've taken you on another wild goose chase."

Bear didn't appear to be listening. "Bracebridge is close to here, isn't it?" He rubbed his belly. "I'm starving. Let's grab a bite at your family's restaurant."

My dad's not a person who's easy to get to know. He used to work up front at the restaurant, chatting with regulars. After my mother died, he started staying behind the scenes to cook, purchase the food and handle the books. His long-time employee, Jeannie, was more than capable of taking charge of the dining room. She always took her position seriously. Decked out in a black skirt and crisp white blouse, her blonde hair rolled into a tight bun, she appeared soft-spoken and courteous. However, as both serving staff and customers had witnessed, she could bring out a tiger side when it was needed. I used to daydream that she and Dad might fall in love and marry. Dad seemed so lonely. But, so far, it had not come to pass. She seemed to keep her life a mystery. We only knew she lived at an undisclosed location out-of-town and drove a rusty Land Rover each day to work.

The prep man in the kitchen was Bruce, whose non-stop task was stuffing potatoes into the massive electric peeler.

Dad refused to buy frozen french fries. The man was a non-stop talker: recapping what was on the news last night, reciting the local gossip picked up at the Riverside Inn bar, or giving a play-by-play of last night's hockey game. For my father, it was white noise. He seldom responded, but just let Bruce ramble on and on.

I was astonished when Dad came out front and removed the menus from our table. "These are not for family and friends. You look like a hungry guy. I'll grill you a nice steak, make a salad. Leave it with me."

Bear wasn't one to be shy. He followed my father into the kitchen, leaving me to look around the restaurant. The walls cried out for a fresh coat of paint and the flooring was worn in pathways from scuffing boots. I counted three booths with torn upholstery. It was high tourist season, yet only two other tables were filled. In the corner, Mr. Mooney, the high school janitor, was reading his newspaper while inhaling his soup. He occupied that table every night. The booth by the door held an older couple I didn't recognize.

Bear couldn't stop raving as he shovelled down his dinner. "Look! I can cut this steak with a butter knife. What do you call this salad?" He insisted my father join us. "The roast potatoes are inspiring. If I wasn't all fed up, I'd eat a mountain more." I saw a smile flash on my father's face. "I don't want to sound pompous and tell you what to do, but you should dump your regular menu and serve your customers this." Bear pointed to his clean plate where he had wiped up the last speck of sauce with a giant hunk of garlic bread.

Jake had hated coming to the restaurant. He was a finicky eater—his body was his temple. He sipped protein drinks, crunched on granola bars, and mixed a ghastly green powder into water with bananas and yogurt. He weighed his food and counted calories, only allowing himself pizza and beer once a week. In hindsight, I realized that his obsession with nutrition and his physique had become annoying. The last Friday night dinner we had shared, I had ordered our traditional pizza with the works. He had put his hand up to stop the waitress. "No, no. Remember, Pen, we are on a new regime. Change that to a small vegetarian and two garden salads, no dressing." He handed the menus back. "By the way, do you have lemon?"

"Forget that," I had complained, addressing the server, who was now tapping her pencil on her pad, her eyebrows raised. "Donna, just kill the second small pizza and make mine a medium with extra cheese and double pepperoni." We spent the rest of dinner not speaking. I drank three beers to his one Coors Light. I ate the pizza crust, which I hated, just to prove my point.

My eyes rested back on my dad. It was hard to believe how much my life had changed since Jake's departure. Bear offered to pay the bill. "What?" my father bellowed. "I'm charging my own daughter for meals now?"

As we left the restaurant, Bear called Marlin. My brother insisted we drop in to see him before we returned to the city. I hesitated, reluctant and somewhat embarrassed for Bear to see where we lived. The restaurant was sad but still normal; our home was out and out odd. But Marlin insisted we check out his new workshop.

As the car headlights hit the drive-in screen, we passed the snack bar house. Bear exclaimed, "Heavens to Murgatroyd. I love this place. You're always full of surprises." He jammed the gearshift into park, lightly punching me on the shoulder.

"Where's Ziska?" Marlin asked, peering inside the car.

"She's with Lucas tonight. We had a mission in Gravenhurst and couldn't leave her sitting in the car."

I had been sceptical about leaving her behind until I saw Lucas sitting on the futon with the dog in his lap. He scratched her on her sweet spot, letting the dog lick his face. "You know sometimes Ziska looks at me, and I swear she's reading my mind," he had said. This from a guy who couldn't remember my name.

My brother wagged a finger at me. "What shenanigans are you up to now?" He shook the sawdust off his baseball cap and led us on a tour of his shed. It looked like a miniature cottage with a front porch and a cupola on the roof. The interior was lined with pegboard where he had organized his tools. He showed us the reclaimed door and windows his boss had donated from a renovation. "Your dream home," I said, laying an arm over his shoulder. "When do you move in?"

My brother ignored my comment. "Hey, Bear. Come look at this." He switched on an exterior light, illuminating the outside back wall. "Here's my dad's shovel collection." We did not have a garage; my dad had previously lined up his shovels by the back door. I had never realized he was such an avid collector. At least twenty shovels of assorted sizes hung on hooks.

"Impressive," Bear said.

I pointed at the big snow scoop hanging off an industrial-size hook. "Marlin, do you remember the winter when Dad pulled us around on this behind the car?"

"Yeah, except you bumped your nose, and Mom found out. She said he was lucky someone didn't call Children's Aid."

Bear looked towards the house. "Is your mother home? I'd like to meet her."

I'm not sure why neither my brother nor I said anything. Marlin changed the subject by handing Bear a piece of grid paper with a drawing of a cupola with louvres. It looked like a miniature pagoda. "What do you think? This is the business I want to get into, once I finish my apprenticeship. I'm working on a ton of new designs."

"If I had a house, I'd buy ten," Bear proclaimed, admiring the details. My brother glowed like a new father.

"When did you get so talented?" I asked. In high school, he had floundered, trying auto shop, then welding, and even culinary class. Every summer, he would have to make up English and math courses to complete his year. I think my dad secretly hoped he'd join him in the food trade. My brother, however, had confided to me that he wanted to work with his hands, but not chopping onions.

While Marlin pulled out a drawer of designs, I mused. If we had the whole weekend, I'd take Bear swimming at High Falls and borrow Dad's boat to tour the lakes. But Bear was due at the bakery by five the next morning.

Before leaving, I slipped into the house and wrapped my mother's ashes in the Christmas tablecloth. I slipped the package onto the floor under the front seat of the car.

Bear and I had a quiet trip back to Toronto. Several times I wanted to tell him about my mother, but I just didn't seem able to talk about it.

"What's our next step?" he asked, turning into the alley behind our apartment building.

I yawned. "Unless Mary Smith still lives on Barton in Hamilton, I think we're scuppered."

"Never say die!" he cried, banging his fist on the steering wheel. "Come over drink night and we'll get on the internet and do some investigating."

"What about your girlfriend?"

He looked at me, confused. "What are you stewing about?"

"I don't want to cause you any grief." Actually, I was concerned. Since her accusations, I had visions of Giselle hiding behind the door, jumping out and shoving me down the stairwell.

"I told you. Giselle loves to be theatrical," he said, opening the car door for me. "No worries."

Eighteen

I wasn't used to hanging out with girls like Giselle. My best friend Kim and I had met on my twenty-third day of high school. I was summoned to the office to guide a new student around the facilities. I did a double-take when I saw this girl standing in the lobby wearing bobby socks and saddle shoes. I scanned her skirt for poodles. With her hair pulled back into a bouncy ponytail, she appeared some sort of throwback from the '50s. What had I signed up for?

A tenth-grader jeered as I led the new girl past the cafeteria, "Hey, Peggy Sue!" She didn't flinch, but stomped up to the offender. "Do you have a problem?" she demanded, grabbing him by the collar. When he didn't answer, she said, "Because I don't give two cents if you do."

I liked this girl from that moment on. This was a person who really didn't care what other people thought. After spending my whole life quaking in my boots, being around her was like popping Valiums. Not that I knew what that was like. But she made me feel calm, cool and collected.

Kim had learned how to sew from her tailor grandfather, becoming adept enough to design her own clothes. I followed her around to fabric stores, helping her sort through boxes of old patterns and yard goods. I would work on our homework, sometimes reading *King Lear* or *Hamlet* out loud while she cut material or ironed. She was inordinately skilled at talking with a mouth full of pins. She looked striking in all her creations. But I always thought what she wore best was her attitude.

My mom and Kim used to giggle together in our living room, collaborating on sewing projects while I did the dishes, stuck in our closet kitchen. Sometimes I felt jealous. Especially the day my mother called her the daughter she never had. Seeing the look on my face, she pinched my cheeks, "Oh don't get all thin-skinned. You know what I mean. The girl knows how to unpick stitches!"

I never fully appreciated my mother's talents until Kim moved to town. My mom didn't help out at the restaurant, but ran her own tailoring business, hemming pants and fixing zippers. She sewed hundreds of wedding dresses. While she pinned or ironed—the ironing board was a fixture in our house—she listened to music. She had an ancient turntable on which she played scratchy records. Bands like Perth County Conspiracy and Crosby, Stills and Nash and folk singers like Eric Andersen and Joan Baez. My dad called it hippie caterwauling.

Other than Halloween costumes, I wouldn't let her make me anything; homemade clothes would just be one more reason for kids to tease me. When Kim raved about how cool it was to have a mother so gifted, I thought her crazy. What about her doctor mother? Everyone in town respected Kim's mom; mine was considered kooky.

Kim's parents were both physicians. The town had seduced new doctors. Their marketing ploy was to push the playground aspect of Muskoka. She told me her dad bought a new set of clubs and a membership at South Muskoka Golf

Club, but because of demands at the hospital, he had yet to play more than three rounds.

We must have looked like a peculiar twosome, Kim in her outrageous self-designed couture-styled dresses and me in my ripped jeans and hoodies. Early on in our friendship, she forced me into her mother's walk-in closet to try on clothes. I stared stupidly and exclaimed, "This closet is bigger than our house," sinking onto a round leather ottoman.

"I come from a long line of clotheshorses," commented Kim, sorting through row after row of hangers.

I felt uneasy. "Maybe we shouldn't be in here." Her mother was a touch snotty. I was pretty sure she didn't like her daughter even spending time at our house. Kim never said so, but I read it in her mother's eyes. Like we might have something contagious. I'm certain she'd reviewed my extensive chart at the hospital and thought my family were lowlifes. Fortunately, Kim's parents' practices were hectic and they were rarely home.

Kim selected a short-sleeved, cotton-candy-coloured blouse. "Take off your shirt."

"What?" I didn't have a bra on. The only one I owned was in the wash. Moreover, with my lack of chest, it was hardly necessary.

She frowned at me. "Do you want me to strip too? Would that make you more comfortable?" I shook my head firmly. "I'm simply giving you a quick course on how to dress for your body shape." She threw the shirt at me and turned to sort through a rack of skirts.

I pulled my t-shirt off and slipped my arms through the sleeves, quickly buttoning the shirt. She flung a skirt in my direction. "What size are your feet?"

"Eight," I answered, dropping my jeans to the floor.

"Good, my mom is 8-1/2." One whole wall towered floor to ceiling with shelves full of shoe boxes. Kim stood on a small ladder and reached up to the top shelf. Each box had a sketch of the shoes inside taped to the end. The wall was a shoe-themed Picasso.

She stood beside me in front of a full-length mirror. I blinked. It reminded me of the hall of mirrors found at amusement parks, except instead of making my reflection look short and squat, I appeared tall, my hips less wide.

She looked smug. "This is no illusion," she said, pulling my hair away from my face. "There is a technique to dressing. See how this A-line skirt accentuates your small waist?" How did she get to be so clever? I admired how the hem was long enough to cover my chubby knees. "And by wearing V-neck shirts, it creates the impression of boobs." We giggled.

"What are you two adolescents up to?" yelled her brother from the hallway.

John was supposed to graduate high school the year we completed Grade Nine. I had a puppy-dog crush on him until I got to know him better. He was always getting into trouble. Once he had urinated in the park in front of the grandstand and was charged with indecent exposure. Then he was caught and charged for drinking underage at a party. From that point on, the OPP followed him around, waiting for him to screw up. He enjoyed messing with the cops by driving extra slow, pretending he was intoxicated and when they pulled him over, he'd blow clean on the breathalyser. This would annoy them so much they'd search the car, looking for contraband. One night, an officer found some white powder in the ashtray. They dragged him down to the station, but when they tested the illicit-looking substance, it turned out to be lime-flavoured Pixy Stix candy.

John loved to drink. But he wasn't a mean drunk, not like some of his friends. He was always good to Kim and me and sometimes, if we begged, he'd give us a couple of beers from his case. He had the ability to pound back twenty-four over the course of a Saturday evening, then top it off with an extra-large pizza from Bill's. At six-foot-five, his wiry frame never gained an ounce despite his colossal intake of pizza, hops and yeast.

After dropping out of high school, John went away for a while, and the family didn't talk about him. Not long after his return, I was invited for dinner and, while passing me the pickled beets, he asked if I wanted him to make me a license plate. His mother turned as red as the vegetable. I answered politely, "No thanks—I don't have a car." I was confused. Kim explained afterwards that he'd been incarcerated in Parry Sound and the license plate comment was his way of telling me, which of course, exasperated his mother no end.

Kim had refused to go out with high school boys. They were simply too uncouth and, in fact, they were her opponents. Excelling at school was what drove her. She signed up for every science and mathematics course offered and exceeded all the geeks in calculus and biology. She was a Brainiac dressed in nylons and sleeveless sheath dresses.

Kim told me she attended nursing school because: a) she liked the uniform and b) her father had said she'd be an excellent nurse. Her mother had been disappointed; she wanted her daughter to follow in her footsteps. Weeks into her first nursing job at the hospital, and with her mother's influence, she started the process to apply to medical school. But then she met Boyd.

Boyd was on the short side, the kind you can't help wanting to cuddle like a puppy. My Hobbit, she called him. They met on the *Segwun*, a steamship that toured the lakes every summer, docking in at Gravenhurst. Kim's mother had given her a single ticket for a sunset cruise for her birthday, admitting to me she never knew what to give her daughter. I felt like telling her she could have asked me, but I didn't. It seemed a ridiculous gift. But it had the strange result of bringing these two together. Even though Boyd drove by the wharf every day of his life, he had never been on the tour boat. On this day, however, his mother had cajoled him into escorting relatives from Scotland on the boat.

As the boat slipped away from the dock, Kim claims, she marched up to Boyd on the upper deck and said, "Hi, I'm your new girlfriend." She told us she'd actually been scrutinizing him for a while and he had hit all five of her qualifiers: humour, height (or lack thereof), humility, patience and affability. Bumping into him this way was perfect. I never knew what to believe when she spouted off such nonsense, but I always admired what my mother would have called her gumption.

After I knew Boyd better, he told me his version of their first meeting. He said it was impossible not to notice this figure standing at the bow. She was wearing an outfit that ladies might have worn when ships first sailed; a floor-length skirt, a high-necked blouse with poofy sleeves, and a flouncy hat the circumference of a bicycle tire. In one hand, she twirled a lacy parasol. At first, he thought she was employed by the boat operators to give the tourist attraction some historical ambiance. But when she turned her attention on him, pointing her umbrella at this head, and announcing loudly that he was her paramour, he was mortified. His cousin-several-times-removed had flicked him on the ear, telling him to go buy his new sweetheart a refreshment. Flummoxed, he escorted her to the bar and they talked non-stop the entire trip. The relatives disappeared down below for dinner.

These days, Boyd was a builder, constructing prefabricated cottages for Super Homes. He sometimes traveled all over the province with the home assembly team, or what Kim called the "total erection squad." When he was away, he would readily admit that he couldn't stop thinking about coming home, and would phone Kim nightly.

Boyd's passion was architecture; Frank Lloyd Wright his god. Before they married, the tables in his room were covered in house plans and piles of books open to diagrams of wind turbines and solar panels. His dream is to build an energy-efficient home without forsaking the façade. Kim envisioned a Cape Cod with a picket fence and a Victorian garden. And he will build it, energy-efficient and all. His devotion to her is never-ending. I know what she sees in him — the qualities I wanted in Jake.

Nineteen

"Beware of Greeks bearing gifts for bears," declared Bear as he opened his door to find me holding a brown liquor store bag and a bag of lemons. Drink night had come. After swigging down two tequila shots we hovered over the computer keyboard. He typed "Mary Smith" in the search bar—and more than seventy million results came up. By adding the word Hamilton, it reduced to a hundred thousand.

"Bingo!" I said, clapping my hands. "Now we're getting someplace."

We tried entering the last name as Smith and the first name as Mary under the 411 Canada website along with the city Hamilton. Two entries came up. How could we be so lucky? I figured on thousands. Bear grabbed the phone and dialled. As he questioned the first person, he shook his head. He called the second number and his face fell again. I knew this wouldn't be easy.

He modified the search to include only the initial M. Sixty-seven listings flashed on the screen. He printed the list and we divvied up the pages. I ran to get my portable phone and to change into track pants. Two hours later, I crossed off the last name. Some had hung up, other lines were busy, or no one answered. We had left twenty-seven messages. The ones I actually talked to knew of no Mary in the family and no one living on Barton. No clues. At the end of the session, Bear poured us another shot and I counted up the definite dead ends on the list.

"Nineteen," I said, licking salt off my hand.

I sighed. Why was I doing this? Jake's mother was having an anxiety attack over her son's lack of communication, but why was I chasing this jerk? He obviously had no interest in contacting me. Me, the person without whom he would never have graduated high school or college. I tossed back another shot and slammed the lemon slice into my teeth, sucking hard.

"I've been thinking," said Bear, fading off, not vocalizing his thought. He started banging away on the keyboard.

The alcohol warmed my throat—my legs felt heavy. I recalled how I had written every one of Jake's essays. In Grade Eleven, he'd been close to failing. If possible, he would have snuck me into his exams too. I studied for him, jotting down key points to help him cram. His marks began to creep up into the seventies. Our English teacher remarked how much better he was on projects than writing tests. You think? But she never seemed to put two and two together. I managed to slide it under the teachers' noses by making sure his essays did not shine, mediocre at best. And it wasn't easy for me to dummy down.

If I had handed in the same paper under my own name, I probably would have received an F. But golden-boy Jake was swamped with compliments and high praise, especially from the female instructors. Stupid me. He then started to use this to his advantage, switching courses to end up with only women teachers.

Bear groaned. I looked over, watching him fervently hunt for a clue. Kim had told him the story of Jake's departure, but he had never questioned my obsession with locating him.

"Do you think we're being completely foolish?" I asked. He stopped typing. "I mean we accepted the bartender's word that this girl's name is Mary Smith. Doesn't it seem too mundane? The guy had to be lying."

Bear shook his head. "Led by our noses down the garden path."

"We're such dopes," I said, holding out my shot glass. "I used to think I was above average intelligence."

He filled it, and raised his high in the air. "To super sleuths, Agatha and Hercules of Riverdale!"

I downed my drink, choking because I forgot the salt and lemon. When I regained my composure, I asked: "Do we go back and coerce that waitress into telling us the truth?"

"Perhaps a ménage-à-trois?" he quipped.

I threw a pillow at his head but misjudged and over-shot—it landed on a pair of golden high heels. I looked up to see a blurry Giselle towering over us. She didn't have to say anything. I felt her stingray eyes piercing my skull. Had she heard Bear's last remark? It had been a joke, but humour was not exactly her oyster.

"Hey, Giselle," he slurred. "Wanna help?"

I didn't wait for her reply. I grabbed my papers and pens and made a speedy exit back to my apartment. I dropped onto my bed, anchoring one foot on the floor, hoping the room would stop spinning, mulling over Bear's girlfriend and his state of affairs. Three nights earlier, I had overheard a conversation through the open kitchen window. I had been in the middle of eating my dinner with a book propped open on the table. When I heard her voice, I had intended to close the window but something stopped me.

She was lecturing Bear on how he needed a better job to move up in the world. She said, "Baking tarts isn't going to buy us a condo in St. Thomas. Have you even put any money away yet?" Her diatribe went on, ad nauseam, while I munched on a smoked meat sandwich and a heap of coleslaw. As I scooped another serving, she began listing the occupations that make the most money. Real estate was an excellent choice, she declared. I had begun to wonder if Bear had fallen asleep or if he was even there. I didn't hear a peep from him. But when her catalogue of high-paying jobs continued and hit dentistry, I heard a roar. Then for a few seconds, all went quiet. I returned to reading, trying to crunch silently on a pickle.

I heard a cupboard door slam and Bear ask: "What's exactly wrong with being a baker?"

"It's fine for a hobby, baby," she insisted. "But really, how much do you make an hour? We can't possibly live on that."

Bear's voice grew louder. "Why don't you go back to school and learn how to pull out teeth? Then I could stay home and bake squares and bring up baby bears."

Giselle exhaled noisily. "Surely this can't be all you want?"

"I've told you already, my dream is to own a little bakery. I've been working on a new light pie crust and a revolutionary cake recipe," he added.

Without a sound, I had placed my dishes into the sink and pulled a mug out of the cupboard. I opened the freezer, scooping mint chocolate ice cream into the coffee cup. Bear's voice softened as he described his vision. I tiptoed over to the window and sat cross-legged on the floor in order to hear him better.

"I see a cozy shop window where I'll display the choicest baked goods. Like artwork." He paused. "Can't you see it? A table covered in a starched white tablecloth where I will place a steaming raspberry pie."

I smiled. I could almost smell the sweetened fruit.

"Are you on crack?" snapped Giselle. "You can't even keep this kitchen clean. How could you run a bakery?"

At that point, I dropped my spoon — it fell, clanging onto the tile floor. I snatched it up and dashed out of the kitchen, finishing up my dessert on the couch.

Twenty

I called John again. I had left several messages on his cell phone. Since he had hired Ginger, he might know her real name and where she came from. I should have called him long ago, but I had been too embarrassed. I decided that if he didn't answer this time, I'd have to resort to contacting Kim — not that I wanted to be cross-examined. She'd be angry about my continued attempts to track down Jake.

No answer. Again, it slipped to voicemail: "Hey, you've reached John, the man of your dreams. Leave me your number and your hotel key and I'll be right there." I had to laugh at his new message. He was stuck in party mode, enjoying less-than-serious relationships. I left message number nine. But as I put the receiver back on the cradle, it immediately rang. I grabbed it.

"John?"

"Pen, it's me, Marlin." My brother's voice sounded off kilter. "I need you to come up here," he said.

My worst fear flew to mind. "What's happening? Is it Dad?"

"God, no," he said, whispering into the phone. "I did a stupid thing."

"What are you talking about? Where are you?" I asked, confused.

"I'm in the bathroom. There's this girl, I don't know what to do."

My brother had had a steady girlfriend in high school, but when she left for university, they had drifted apart. He had dated a few others since but no one he had clicked with.

Why was he hiding in the bathroom? I whispered back, "What girl?"

"I've been chatting with someone on the internet for months now," he replied. I heard the water running as if he were trying to disguise our conversation. "We seemed to have a lot in common."

My mind raced fast forward. "She came for a surprise visit?"

"How did you know? A week or so ago, we revealed our names. I hadn't even told her where I lived. This afternoon, she knocked on our door."

For a moment, all I could think of was how this person was much more adept at finding someone than I was.

"What am I going to do?"

My curiosity was piqued. "What's she like?"

He sighed. "I don't know. I mean, she's nice."

"Where's she from?"

"She landed here on the bus from B.C. with what looks like all her worldly goods."

"Does Dad know?"

"Nope, he's still at the restaurant."

I began to think my brother was overreacting. Was the situation really that dire? "Why don't you bring her down here for a few days?"

I heard him sigh with relief. "Sis?"

"Yeah?"

"Don't listen to anyone else. You're not half bad."

When Marlin arrived with the girl from Salmo, the word *waif* came to mind. She politely slipped off her shoes, leaving them next to mine. I noted that they were half the size of my sandals. Her name was Itsy, which seemed appropriate. I pushed back a burning desire to ask to see her birth certificate. After shaking my hand, she described her arduous journey riding a Greyhound bus across country. I asked if she was hungry — she nodded. I heated up a bowl of leftover spaghetti. She wolfed it down. Within minutes the girl was sound asleep on my sofa.

Marlin and I stared at her in silence.

Finally, I asked: "How old is she?"

"She swears she's twenty-one. You can see why I didn't know what to do. I kept expecting the Mounties to show up accusing me of baiting minors over the internet."

Itsy was clutching a purse; it was hot pink and covered in orange flowers. My brother and I locked eyes. It looked like something only a teenybopper would buy. Could we trust her? Maybe she was a runaway. She snored and rolled onto her side, tucking her legs into the fetal position. Ziska was fascinated with this new arrival, sniffing and snorting and attempting to cuddle with her. I had to resort to locking the dog in her crate. She looked out at us with big sad eyes.

"Itsy's cute," Marlin mused, as if she were a puppy.

I rolled my eyes.

We left her sleeping on the couch and I pulled out a sleeping bag and opened it on the living room rug. I let Marlin use my room. When I woke, Itsy was in the kitchen making coffee, with Ziska sitting at attention on a chair. With my eyes only half open, I picked up the dog, placed her on the floor and sat down at the table. A passport was propped open by the sugar bowl.

She poured coffee into a mug. "I was pretty wiped yesterday. I hardly slept a wink on that bus. I'm sure I wasn't making a whole lot of sense last night." She sat with her legs tucked under her on the chair, her hands cradling her cup. "People never believe me when I tell them my age. I guess it's my button nose and my big brown eyes." She batted her eyelashes.

"Oh, we believed you," I said, picking up the passport and holding it up to compare her face with the photo. I read the birth date aloud. "Yup, no problem here, we were totally convinced."

Itsy laughed loudly, splattering coffee onto her shirt.

Marlin stumbled into the room, one leg in his jeans. "What's going on?"

By my calculations, it took my brother fewer than twenty-four hours to fall in love. Bear knocked on the door at nine and asked if I wanted to go to the Ex. He thumped my brother on the back. "Fish, good to see you. The more the merrier. Let's hit the road." Eyeing Itsy, he added: "And who do we have here?"

"What's the Ex?" asked Itsy.

"Just the biggest and best fair in the whole country. Rides, tasty food, cows." Bear gave me a playful punch in the shoulder.

The Ex gang included Lucas and Bear's girlfriend Giselle. She was dressed in a miniskirt and stilettos which I categorized as totally inappropriate attire. We had to slow our pace so she could keep up with us while we walked from the streetcar stop to the exhibition gates. It was painful to watch.

We bought all-day passes. But after one ride, Giselle refused to participate. She had broken a heel jumping from the swing ride. Bear tried to woo her onto the Tilt-A-Whirl but she pushed him away. At lunch, Lucas ate a sausage loaded with sauerkraut and onions, two deep-fried Twinkies, pasta in a cup, an apple fritter and two snow-cones at the Food Building. Then he complained of feeling queasy and he began sitting out the rides as well.

In the afternoon, dark clouds blew in; rain threatened, and as a result the line-ups grew shorter. The four of us ran from ride to ride. Marlin grabbed Itsy's hand and lunged into a seat on the Ferris wheel. I watched them whirl up into the air, my brother talking a mile a minute, his new friend laughing. He put his arm around her.

"What are you grinning about?" asked Bear.

"It's so great to see two people really enjoying one another," I said, climbing onto the seat.

"Itsy is the cat's meow," Bear said.

The operator pushed the safety bar down and we bobbed forward and up. As we swung above the midway, the aroma of popcorn, cotton candy and beer nuts hit my nostrils.

Our car lifted upwards, swinging gently, as more passengers were loaded. I looked down at the mob of people going in every direction. When we were only half way to the top of the wheel, my throat tightened. I saw a blond head in the crowd below—and somehow, I knew it was Jake. Although his facial features weren't clear, the black jeans, plain white tailored shirt, and long sleeves characteristically rolled to just below his elbows made me hold my breath. He stopped just below the Ferris wheel. Then he turned. It was Jake. I grabbed Bear's arm. "Look! That's him!"

"Who?" asked Bear, hanging his head over the bar and causing our car to rock. "Where?" He had never seen my ex-boyfriend except in a photo. I don't know why I expected him to recognize the guy.

I pointed, stabbing the air with my index finger. "Jake!" I rattled the bar, squirming. Our car began to pitch, swinging us up and down. I yelled, hand around my mouth. "Let us down!"

Bear grabbed my hand, his face turning green. "Pen, stop! Unless you want regurgitated pizza in your lap."

I stared down into the fairgrounds. Jake stood in front of a game, the one where you pound a hammer and ring a bell. He swung and the woman at his elbow clapped her hands. The carny waved his hand across a wall of prizes. Then he turned to the brunette. Her face was obscured — only the top of her head was visible. She pointed to a stuffed snake. I rattled the bar harder. I had to get off this thing. Just my luck. I screamed to Marlin in the car above, but the music, distant cries from the people on the roller coaster, and the ding, ding, ding of the games below muffled my cries.

Bear grabbed my arm again but I ignored him. Jake and Lady Number Two were walking into the crowd, moving toward the exhibit buildings. The rat had been gone less than six weeks and he'd already moved on to a second woman. First a blonde, now a brunette. I banged my hands on the metal crossbar in frustration, watching helplessly as they passed the dour-faced Giselle and sad-sack Lucas sitting on a bench before vanishing into a tent.

The Ferris wheel began to rotate — now we were stuck up at the top. I could see Lake Ontario with sailboats skimming across the water. I was a prisoner to the view.

Bear tried to calm me down. "Don't worry. We'll get off soon and check out the tents and buildings."

I frowned. It was useless. The likelihood of finding the pair was next to nil. The list of things I was going to say to Jake, the speech rehearsed a thousand and two times, rang in my head. The spineless son of a bitch. Most men would have the decency to break up in person.

For the rest of the day, I continued to scan the crowd for sandy-haired males. Marlin tried to reassure me, telling me that at least I could tell his mother he was alive and well and only two hours away. But now I wasn't sure. Was it really Jake? With a new woman to boot? Nothing made any sense.

Once we disembarked from the Ferris wheel, I fell behind, allowing Itsy and Marlin to walk ahead, hand in hand. Hours before, I had savoured the rush of the rides like a nine-year-old, but after seeing Jake, I felt tired and out of sorts.

To top it off, the gray clouds released and we were doused by sheets of rain. Itsy laughed and jumped over the puddles. Despite my frame of mind, I knew I was beginning to like this glass-half-full girl. My shirt was stuck to my skin as we rode the Red Rocket, our last ride of the day. The only saving grace was seeing how wretched Giselle looked, her mascara running down to her chin, shoes in hand and bare feet filthy.

As we zoomed from one subway stop to the next, Itsy revealed that her father was an unemployed logger and her mother ran a daycare centre. Salmo, the town where she grew up, did not have a lot to offer in terms of employment. For a year, she had driven into Nelson to work at a factory, but the company had recently closed up shop. She was the youngest of seven kids, all still living at home. She had shared an attic room with three sisters. When she lost her job, she decided it was time to move out.

Twenty-One

While Itsy changed into dry clothes back at the apartment, Marlin told me she had apologized to him for showing up unannounced. She'd been afraid that if she asked, he would have said no, and she was desperate for a jumping-off point. She didn't want him to worry, thinking she was some crazy girl who was going to camp out on his doorstep and expect him to take care of her. She'd figure out what to do next and where best to look for a job. Ontario would be a good place to make a fresh start.

Bear insisted we order in Chinese food for dinner. His treat. When we squeezed around his table, Giselle snuggled up beside him, hardly touching her food. Itsy dove into a container of General Tso's chicken and then finished off the honey garlic ribs, licking her fingers. Marlin watched her, his eyes lighting up. I felt it too. There was something infectious about being with someone who relished every second of life. My frame of mind swung a hundred and eighty degrees again. I asked Lucas to open more wine, dumping a gigantic scoop of beef and broccoli on top of my vegetable fried rice.

Near midnight, when I returned to my dark apartment, I noticed the blinking red light on my phone. When I picked it up, there was finally a message from John, telling me to call him right away, regardless of the hour. I dialled, listening to it ring expecting John's cocky message.

"Hey there, Pen," said a voice. "Sorry I didn't get back to you but I lost my cell phone in a bar and I only got it back today."

With John, you had to get right to the point. He had a way of talking in circles before you realized it. "Jake's mother is having a stroke," I said. "I'm helping her look for him." Why was I justifying myself? "Do you have any clue where he is or what this Ginger girl's real name is?" I continued. I could hear cackles in the background and the squeaking of a bedspring.

John's voice was muted as if his palm was covering the phone. "Hey, Polly, do you know Ginger's real name?"

I felt my face flush. Had I caught him in the sack with someone? I could only hear inaudible discussion. It went on for a few minutes and I started to wonder if he'd forgotten about me.

Marlin and Itsy teetered into the room, returning from next door, laughing, oblivious to me as I had yet to turn on the light. He picked her up and carried her over the threshold into the bedroom.

Suddenly John's voice rang in my ear. "Are you still there? Sorry, I had to explain the situation. Polly is super guarded about those girls."

I tightened my grip on the phone. Was Polly our waitress, I wondered?

"She says a couple came in last week asking questions," John explained. "Was that you?"

I nodded to myself. Polly was definitely our well-endowed, tight-lipped server.

"Yes, yes. Does she know anything?" I blurted out, stretching to turn the floor lamp on.

"The dancers don't always tell the straight goods," he said. "And the bar protects their investment, so to speak."

What was he babbling on about? I just need to know if he had any information.

"All she knows is that Ginger hails from Stoney Creek." I grabbed my notebook from the coffee table. "And she's studying to become a physiotherapist."

My mental brakes came screeching to a halt. I had assumed her to be a flake, some dumb blonde. "Does Polly know where she's going to school?"

There was a pause — then a female voice came over the line. "I apologize for being rude the other night, but you must understand I can't divulge information, or these girls wouldn't work for me again. Ginger is different than most. She's dancing her way through university." I liked this euphemism for stripping. It sounded much nicer, like every night she got up and did a snappy tap shoe routine with tails and a top hat.

"Can you think of anything else that might help me find her?" I asked.

"She said something about Master. Master University?"

"McMaster?" I'd seen the school on the map of Hamilton.

"That's right. I know she was ecstatic because this was her last summer to work at the club. Then she just took off with some guy. The only thing I recall her talking about was being raised by a single mom, a hairdresser. That's where she learned about makeup and hair extensions."

After thanking her profusely, I hung up the phone and sat pondering these new clues. How do you get a list of students from a university? Where was this Stoney Creek place and how big was it? Would I have to check out a thousand hair salons to find her mother?

Just then, Marlin opened the bedroom door, shutting it quietly behind him. He bounced down onto the couch. I had never seen him in such high spirits.

I elbowed him. "I don't know. I'm a bit worried about you rushing into this relationship," I said.

He grinned, leaning back, crossing his arms behind his head. "We're going to take it slow."

"I really do like her," I admitted.

He sat upright and tapped me on the knee. "Doesn't she remind you a bit of Mom?" I felt my eyes filling up when he looked away. When he spoke, he was crying too. "Is that too weird? Do I have some sort of Oedipus complex?"

"She's not Mom. She just has a spirit like her," I said. "You can't help being drawn to someone with such joie de vivre."

Marlin ran his fingers through his hair. "Is it possible to fall in love in one day?"

I laughed. "I thought you were taking it easy?"

He then changed the subject, asking: "Who were you on the phone with?"

While I made coffee, I told him about how Bear and I were checking into the whereabouts of Jake. He listened to the whole story without comment. Then he handed me the milk. "Why are you doing this?"

"For his mother."

Marlin pointed his spoon at me. "Give her the information and let her look into it."

"You don't understand."

"Yes, I do. I told you not to become involved in Boyd's stag. I regret helping to make that stupid cake." He shook his head. "But there's no excuse for Jake running off with that woman. Not without one word to you or his mother. He owes both of you more than that."

"Maybe it was my fault," I offered, sipping my coffee.

Marlin was silent, his lips pressed together. "Is that what you think?" He slammed his mug down on the table.

I nodded.

Even in the dull light, I could see his face go dark red. "Let the jackass go. It's over, don't you see?"

I stared into my mug. "I will. I just have to see him, know he's all right."

"But you saw him today — wasn't he in one piece?"

"Was it really him?" I felt shaky as if I was still riding the roller coaster.

Marlin sighed. "You've been impossible to talk to for the last few months. Don't you see now? I tried to tell you Jake's real nature but you refused to listen to any criticism. Kim didn't know what to do either. You shut us out."

The last year was starting to seem like a dream. Had I really turned a deaf ear to everyone?

"What would you say if you did find him?" asked Marlin.

I cleared my throat, about to recite my speech. But I was completely worn out. I put my head down on the kitchen table.

When I awoke, Itsy's bags were at the door. I leapt to my feet. Where was she going? I had already decided to suggest she share my apartment. Surely, she could find work in the city and help me with the rent. I found her and Marlin in the kitchen. She was buttering toast.

"What's going on?" I asked.

Marlin put his cell phone down on the table. "We talked to Dad. Itsy is going to take over as dishwasher. The summer guy quit last night." Itsy beamed as if she'd been offered an executive position at Bombardier.

I slumped down onto a kitchen chair. I had been looking forward to having her company and before I could offer her my place, she was leaving. Seeing my downcast face, my brother wrapped an arm across my shoulder. "You and Bear should get together."

I pushed him away. "He's not my type—besides he's with Giselle." I picked up Ziska and cuddled her on my lap.

"Who, little Miss Fortune Hunter?" Itsy said, wiping greasy fingers on a napkin. "No, that relationship is gasping its last breath."

I shook my head. "You only just met them—she's a bit difficult but..."

Itsy interrupted. "I have a sixth sense. He's in love with you."

I bounced out of my chair. "No, he's not," I sputtered. "We're friends, that's all."

Itsy looked amused, putting her plate and cup in the sink. She turned on the water.

"Leave them," I said. "You two might as well get on the road."

"Well, just forget about Jake and concentrate on the article you're writing," Marlin said, giving me a big hug. I had told them about my personal essay and had interviewed Itsy the previous morning. Her answers were so refreshing. She had zero issues with her body. Something I could only wish for.

I decided my brother was right. My day job wasn't going to satisfy me for long. My paycheque covered the basics, but I needed more. I had felt guilty when Bear paid for the feast of take-out food. He was always paying. I decided it was time to publish or live on Kraft dinner forever. After Marlin and Itsy left, I called Kim with the intention of interviewing her for the article.

She was forthright. "Do you actually want Jake back?"

I didn't feel like being lectured. "You talked to John?"

"You must be psychic. I was about to call you," she said. "As a friend, I've been wrong, but now I'm telling you to stop this nonsense right this second. I don't believe this story about helping his mother track him down. Why are you chasing after him?"

"He was my boyfriend for six years. I thought we'd get married."

"You believed that?" asked Kim, her voice growing in intensity. "Where have you been?"

I slammed the phone down.

Twenty-Two

I fed Ziska, dressed in thirty-eight seconds, and then, flinging open the apartment door, ran smack into Bear. He almost dropped the plate he was holding.

"Where's the fire?" he asked, flamboyantly swinging the tray of pastry under my nose. "You've gotta try my new lemon tart recipe."

I simply couldn't speak. I rushed past him and dashed down the stairs.

"They're not that bad!" I heard him yell. "Pen, what's the matter?"

I had relied on Bear far too much—it was endangering his relationship with Giselle. I was determined to continue my search for Jake alone. I had googled Stoney Creek on the computer earlier. It made sense. It was a suburb of Hamilton and Barton Street ran through it too. McMaster University was located on the other side of the city. Everything was coming together. I looked up hair salons along Barton and had jotted down addresses and phone numbers.

The new school year would not begin for a week. Hanging around McMaster wouldn't make any sense at this point. But I could pretend to be writing an article about physiotherapy and ask the office for a contact list of students. My mind swirled with ideas.

I dug out the train schedule from the bottom of my purse and checked my cash. I didn't have to work until the following afternoon so it was the perfect time to head to Hamilton. I was pumped until I discovered I was at the wrong gate at Union Station. I missed the first train. Still determined, I bought a newspaper, and waited. As the next train finally rattled out of the station I stared out the window. "Trains to the left of me, trains to the right," I adlibbed in my head as I improvised the lyrics to *Stuck in the Middle with You.*

What would my mother have done in these circumstances? I bit my lip. She'd never be in this position. I had inherited my mother's body type, but she had a different outlook on life. I cursed her for my hips. And then I saw a reflection of my face in the window as another train passed terrifyingly close. Damn my father and his big nose. Of all the women I'd interviewed, I topped them all when it came to a negative body image.

As the train whizzed by industrial yards I saw an abandoned graffiti-covered building with a menacing cartoon mouse mimicking "Cheese, please." My mother had loved cheese. Is that what had cruelly caused her stroke? Then another realization came to me. Jake's mom, Ann, had not replaced my mother, but we had slowly forged an emotional attachment. It felt strange to be ripped so unexpectedly from his family. I missed the Sunday night dinners, his grandmother's cooking and his grandfather stealing peas out of the pot.

I was relieved when the train finally reached its destination. I focussed on finding the city bus terminal. It only occurred to me when riding the bus to Stoney Creek that my plan was flawed. What if I did have a dozen addresses for beauty shops — even some on Barton? Who was I supposed to ask for when I got there? Should I call out: "Is anyone working here the mother of an exotic dancer?"

I hiked along Barton and into the first hairdressing establishment on my list, asking if anyone had a daughter, possibly with the name Ginger.

No one even looked mildly interested. The second salon had an out-of-business sign taped to the window. At the third, a girl washing a man's hair turned off the water. "That's an odd name. Like on Gilligan's Island?"

I nodded. She waved at the balding male stylist who was blow drying a client's hair, yelling above the sound of the dryer. "Bingo, do any of your employees have a daughter named Ginger?"

The man looked exasperated, and turned off the blow dryer. "You're my only employee."

I checked out two more hairdressers, but my spirit was starting to fade. Thinking about my mother and Jake's family had made me melancholy. With all the walking and the heat, my legs were rubbing together, now making each step agony. I ignored the cost and took a taxi back to the train station.

Later that night, I soaked in a cool bath at home. The phone rang as I wrapped myself in a towel but I didn't answer it. It was Kim. I let it go to voicemail. I felt guilty and then listened to my other messages: one from Bear, another from my dad, one from Jake's mother and a second call from Bear. I ignored them all. Over the next few days, Bear knocked several times but I hid in the bathroom. I even refrained from watching a DVD or listening to music in case it could be heard through the door. For some reason, Ziska didn't even react to the knocking. It was as if she knew we were not to be disturbed. I carried her in my arms when she asked to go out, quietly running up and down the stairs. I crept out early for work and skulked back in at night.

With no ambient noise, I heard the neighbours on the other side fighting. They probably fought every night but I'd never noticed. This was the couple who had watched Marlin from the safety of their peephole the first day I moved in. I'd never actually seen them but I had learned to recognize their voices. One had a high squeaky voice—I think it was the man because every so often I heard him yell, "Damn bitch!"—while the other usually answered by throwing things. One night, I almost called the police. It sounded like they were murdering each other. Then I heard the thump of their bed frame rhythmically hitting our mutual wall.

Twenty-Three

I turned out to be the worst clerk they had ever hired at Honest Ed's. I couldn't fold clothes properly. My supervisor had already written me up for bad form. I swear the customers knew and messed up all my bins and shelves. I was relieved when I was assigned to men's underwear and socks. No folding involved. Every day, a customer came in asking where the tire section was. No matter how many times I explained that we don't sell tires, he kept coming back. My co-worker, Mimi, called him my suitor. I was breaking open another carton of boxer shorts when she popped her head around the corner. "You missed lover boy yesterday," she teased.

I stuck my tongue out.

I decided to ask Mimi out for lunch, wondering if she'd consent to an interview for my body image essay. After I described the purpose, she readily agreed. When I began by asking her age, I was astounded to find out she was near retirement. This is a woman who spent the day scampering up and down ladders. Although she has laugh lines, her face is predominantly wrinkle-free.

We were sitting on bar stools in the window of the pizza parlour. I picked off a slice of pepperoni and popped it in my mouth. Wiping my hand on a napkin, I pulled a pencil from behind my ear. "Have you ever been on a diet? And if so, at what age?"

Mimi chuckled. "What diet have I not been on is more to the question."

I raised my eyebrows. She didn't appear to have an ounce of excess fat anywhere.

She dug into her purse. "Look!" It was a tattered photograph of a woman lounged across a sofa, her fleshy arms holding a baby. Only Mimi's beaked nose was recognizable. "After my kids were born, I hit four hundred and ten pounds. They had to staple my stomach or I would have died."

"That's unbelievable," I said, handing back the dog-eared snapshot.

Mimi threw half of her pizza slice into the garbage. "Now I can only eat tiny meals."

"Do you remember when you first dieted?"

She paused, clamping her eyes shut. "Let me see, my mother put me on a diet in Grade Five. That's right—I was in Miss Oliver's class and the principal phoned my mother concerned because my lunch consisted of carrot and celery sticks."

I looked up from my notebook. "What? How overweight were you?"

"I was skinnier than Twiggy. Do you remember her?" I nodded. Kim had dressed like the legendary '60s model one year for Halloween, drawing cartoon-like lashes under her eyes.

Mimi sipped her club soda. "Well, my mother decided she had to diet, and insisted I join her. She convinced me we were both fat. She was so paranoid about gaining an ounce that I went the other way and ate myself silly. I'd sneak food at night; I stole money to buy chips and chocolate bars after school, devouring them before she came home from work. When I started to look more like a blueberry than a teenager, she banished me to a fat farm. But I ran away the second night and hitchhiked to my grandmother's house. I gained forty pounds that summer."

I was shocked at her mother's behaviour, but stammered out my next question. "Is there a part of your body you love?"

She giggled and slipped off her shoes. "My feet. See how perfect my toes are?" I admired her manicured toenails. "That's my one vice now. I treat myself to a pedicure at least once a month."

"Is there any part of your body you'd like to change?"

"I used to hate every inch of it when I was heavy. My husband used to say—just more of you to love—bless his heart. He died five years ago." She paused.

I glanced up from taking notes, to see her smiling.

"But if I had to pick something, I'd have to say I hate my elbows. My grandkids say they're too pointy."

I detoured from my normal questions. "How many children do you have?"

Mimi broke into a wide grin. "Two daughters. Born exactly two years apart."

"How did you handle the whole body issue with them?"

Mimi brushed the crumbs off our table into her napkin. "You know that's funny. Unlike my mother, I was very careful what I said to Nancy and Elena. I didn't want them to be like me. I told them how perfect they were and always prepared healthy food. But both of them still thumbed through magazines for the latest fad diets. Why do you think that was?"

I tapped my pencil on the table. "My mother said the same to me—you're beautiful as you are. But how could I believe her when I looked in the mirror?" I could hear the bitterness creeping into my voice as I described how ugly I was as a child. "Not to mention, the kids at school who were loath to let me forget."

Mimi squeezed my hand. "Well, you're certainly not ugly now. Besides, beauty is only skin deep. And you're such a kind person. Your mother is right, and she must be very proud of you."

I quickly changed the subject. "Tell me about the stomach operation and the impact it has had on your life."

Mimi talked while I scribbled down notes. We were late returning from our lunch break, and our supervisor shot us a look.

Twenty-Four

That evening, I ran up the stairs from the third to the fourth floor with my keys in hand. I really didn't want to meet anyone in the hall. A small gift bag hung from my apartment doorknob.

I unlocked the door, and in the safety of my apartment, I opened the present. Inside was a kazoo with a note wrapped around it. It read: *Pen – I haven't heard from you in a while. Hope all is tickety-boo. Learn how to play a musical instrument by joining me and the band (just Lucas) tonight at 8 p.m. Your buddy, Bear.*

I laughed out loud. Leave it up to him to break the spell. Damn it. Why let Jake or Giselle ruin my new friendships?

It wasn't too long before the jam session was in full swing across the hall. Lucas was excellent on the bongos. I was pathetic on the kazoo, but so was Bear. He had picked up a whole bag of them at the dollar store.

"Lucas wrote a song," he announced.

"I hope it's better than your bear tune," I added.

He grinned, strumming the guitar with a pick. "Barely."

Lucas smoothed a wrinkled sheet of paper. "It's called *Bad Habits*."

I'll pick up my smelly socks
Wash up the dishes in the sink
Chuck out the newspapers
Febreze my shoes to hide the stink

My man habits
I'll amend, I'll suspend
Nothing I won't do… for you…

I'll put down the toilet seat
Empty the garbage can
Replace the toilet roll
And even turn on the fan

My man habits
I'll amend, I'll suspend
Nothing I won't do… for you…

I'll stop picking my nose
Won't flick it on the floor
Pull the hair from the drain
And start shutting the bathroom door

My man habits
I'll amend, I'll suspend
Nothing I won't do… for you…

I'll toss out the pizza boxes
Recycle those rancid cans
Take out the garbage bin
Scrub the pots and pans

Nothing, nothing, nothing I won't do for you…

I clapped enthusiastically, stifling laughter. For a few terrifying seconds, I wondered if he'd written it for me. But he never looked up, not even for a second. He didn't seem even aware of my presence. I was safe. I relaxed, enjoying his lyrics.

Lucas looked sheepish. "Did you really like it?"

I nodded. What was I going to say? I wondered about the poor girl who was the object of his infatuation. It was interesting how only a few weeks ago, I couldn't keep my eyes off him. And now he seemed downright unattractive. Was it because of his personality or lack thereof? Bear had informed me that Lucas had girlfriends like McDonald's had new menus.

After this musical interlude, I started feeling more like myself. I called Jake's mom Ann to tell her about the possible sighting of Jake and my lack of progress. She was still worried but somewhat relieved. She'd also just returned from the post office where she picked up a postcard from Niagara Falls. It had no return address and simply stated: *Don't worry. I am fine and will call you soon. Jake.*

"It definitely looks like his handwriting. But it still doesn't make sense," she insisted. "Why would he run off with this other woman? Is there something you're not telling me?"

I felt my face flush. I wanted to answer, "Yes, your son's an asshole," but instead I stoically replied, "I'm as perplexed as you are."

"When you come to visit your family next time, promise you'll come over for dinner," she said, signing off. I agreed but knew I wouldn't.

I called Dad. He sounded cheerful, telling me Itsy was a good little trouper. "When are you coming home again?" he asked. "And are you bringing your new boyfriend with you?"

I sighed. "Dad, how many times do I have to tell you? Bear is not my boyfriend."

I hung up, leaping from the couch. Ziska looked up at me with her death stare. "I know, I know. I'll call Kim back too." I picked the phone up and was mulling over what to say to my best friend when a loud knock sounded on my apartment door. I put an eye up to the peephole and couldn't believe my eyes. Kim and Boyd were standing there on my new "Go Away" doormat. I threw open the door.

Before I could utter a word, Kim pushed inside. "We've come to kidnap you," she said, escorting me into the bedroom. "Get dressed. We're going on a picnic. Pack a bathing suit and a toothbrush."

"I can't. I have a shift at eleven," I argued, wondering why you would need a toothbrush on a picnic.

She crossed her arms. "Too bad," she said. "Call work and tell them you can't make it." She put a hand on my forehead. "Definitely sick. What do you think, Boyd?"

He picked up my address book and flipped through the pages. "I'll call and say I'm your father. I'll tell them you're deathly ill and it's coming out both ends."

I ripped the book from his hands. "Okay, okay. I'll dump my shift," I said, "but what about Ziska?"

"What about your new neighbours I've heard so much about?" asked Boyd.

"Good idea," said Kim. She pulled out an overnight bag from my closet and tossed it towards me. "Get ready. I'll check to see if Bear will take care of the dog."

"Forget it—he's at the bakery every morning," I lied, knowing he never worked weekends.

"Too bad," said Kim, smiling at Boyd. "I wanted you to meet him. I'll see if Lucas is home."

Lucas answered the door and agreed to care for Ziska. "Hey, buddy," he said crouching down beside her. "How about a walk in the park? Maybe get some street meat, check out the action. You're not into those skanky little Chihuahuas, are you?"

When we stepped out the lobby doors, Bear was leaning on the railing in front of the building, a devilish grin on his face. I should have known better. It was a conspiracy. He stuck out his hands pretending to be handcuffed. "I've never been kidnapped before."

Kim drove—Boyd complained for fourteen and a half blocks about her city driving abilities.

"Bear," she said, glancing in the rear-view mirror. "Any suggestions on how we can shake this Jake fixation out of the girl?"

"A blind date with a mysterious stranger?" he replied.

"Where are we going?" I demanded.

"On a Niagara wine tour," drifted a voice from the front seat.

I smiled.

On the way, Boyd and Bear sang all the songs from *The Sound of Music* and had just started on *Jesus Christ Superstar* when we pulled off the highway and down a long dirt road to our first winery.

Twenty-Five

Fast forward sampling at three wineries, and as you might imagine, not one of us was fit to drive. As luck would have it, the vintner at our last stop contacted a friend and found a couple of rooms — no small feat in high season. He loaded us into a cab and sent us off to a bed and breakfast on the outskirts of Niagara-on-the-Lake. As we arrived at our destination, the manager swung open the front door and announced that it was his last weekend; he was quitting and moving to Manhattan. To our chagrin, this prompted the Bear and Boyd duet again and they began to croon the *Green Acres* theme song.

The man doubled over with laughter. "I like you two," he said, putting his arm around the guys. He gave us a tour of the kitchen, informing us we could eat anything we wanted. He didn't care. He usually only served breakfast but we might as well eat up. He'd be gone by Sunday night.

I sat on a bar stool at the kitchen island and watched as my abductors prepared a meal. Boyd unearthed two boxes of crackers, slicing cheese into perfect squares. Bear whisked eggs, then chopped green onions and mushrooms. He found a pan in the dish rack and poured in the egg mixture, shoving it into the oven. Kim had purchased a case of wine, but it took her ten minutes to select one from the dozen bottles. She proceeded to open every drawer and cupboard looking for the corkscrew.

"You'd think a B&B in wine country would have a drawer full," she said. "All they have is this plastic opener and it looks like it was stolen from the Watergate Hotel."

We all laughed; and thereafter seemed to be amused by everything we said or did. I couldn't remember the last time I felt so utterly silly—my sides ached from laughter. After we gobbled down the cheese and crackers, we ate dinner, scraping the egg pan clean.

Kim and Boyd snuck off while I was loading the dishwasher. This left Bear and me to share the small downstairs bedroom. It was not one of the rooms normally rented out but a closet-sized spare room for the staff, simply furnished with a three-quarter bed.

"I'll crash in the living room," he said, picking up his overnight bag.

"No, it was my friends that got you into this predicament. I don't mind—I'll sleep out on the couch," I said.

He shook his head. "It's early. Other guests may be coming in and might disturb you. You take the bed."

I took a step towards the door. Suddenly, my head started spinning. We had consumed a lot of wine. I plopped down on my suitcase.

Bear pulled me to my feet and helped me into the bedroom. "We both need sleep. You take this side and get under the blankets. I'll sleep on top of the covers on the other side. Agreed?" I nodded. The sheets were calling to me, my head petitioning the pillow. He yanked the quilt back and tucked me in. He switched off the light. I must have fallen instantly into a dream as I heard someone whisper, "Goodnight, my lucky Penny."

I woke in the middle of the night, my mouth parched. The blankets had slipped off but I was still warm. Bear was cuddled up to my backside, his arm around my waist. I fell back asleep.

When I opened my eyes next, he was gone from the room. The heady smell of frying bacon and baked bananas wafted into the room. I followed my nose and found him cooking breakfast while the manager sat on a stool chatting and sipping coffee.

"I'm making my famous banana pancakes," he proclaimed. "Most people aren't vigilant with the proportions and they become far too gummy."

"Are bananas good for babies?" asked Kim, entering behind me with a sleepy Boyd in tow.

I grabbed her by the shoulders. "Are you pregnant?" I asked.

She laughed. "Do you think I'll be a good mother?"

"Of course," I stuttered.

"Boo!" She gave me a hip check. "I'm not having a baby. Yet. Got you going for a second, right?" Whispering in my ear, she added: "How was the hibernation?"

I pinched her hard on the back of her arm.

Twenty-Six

We lingered around the breakfast table, sipping lukewarm coffee. I don't know why, but I started talking about my mother. I rambled on and on, but no one interrupted.

The summer I turned eleven, my mother had said I was old enough to go on one of her explorations. Every year she packed up our station wagon and would take off for parts unknown alone. She said it rejuvenated her.

One year she taped a map of Ontario to the kitchen wall, found a push pin, covered her eyes with a dishtowel and had us spin her around. It was like grown-up pin-the-tail-on-the-donkey. The pin landed smack dab on the city of London.

The following year she went to Paris. Paris, Ontario that is. The next summer she drove all the way to Rome, New York. But the year I turned eleven she spread out the tattered map and exclaimed, "This year we're off to Athens together." I was thrilled!

I packed my new jellybean sandals, my bathing suit, an emerald green nightie and six books in my olive-green suitcase. Mom made me remove five of the books and put in shorts, underwear and a fancy dress for dinner.

I was big enough to sit in the front seat and was the official navigator. I studied the map as she drove out of town and announced our choices — the big highway or the back roads.

She insisted we avoid Toronto like the plague. So...back roads it was.

It took us the better part of the day to reach Athens. I remember driving around lakes, through dozens of towns, winding across cottage country into farmland, through forests and around fields of corn and cows. We stopped at a picnic area by a river and spread out our lunch. I was fascinated by the radishes Mom had painstakingly cut into flowers.

Nearing Athens, I could hardly contain myself. We'd been gabbing about the real Greece, the Parthenon and even the Olympics. Mom started talking animatedly about Ireland and how green it was. She promised to take me there after I finished college. All of a sudden, I yanked on her sleeve. We had missed Athens!

Doing an immediate and faultless U-turn, she drove back into the village. Sure enough, a sign over the fire hall confirmed it. We stopped. Mom snapped a picture of me standing on the hood of the car, pointing up at the sign. Athens seemed kind of quiet and boring, even compared to Bracebridge. But now that we'd arrived, we decided to grab a quick drink at a local restaurant.

I remember Mom chatting to the waitress. She was always engaging people in conversation—before they knew it, she would magically extract their life story. The waitress eagerly asked if we'd seen the town's murals. So we took a walking tour. On one building was an old-fashioned picture of a train station with ladies in long dresses beside a horse and cart. On the firehall was a mural of men throwing buckets of water at a burning building. Athens, Ontario may not have boasted the art of ancient Greece, but I had to admit the murals were really quite riveting.

I thought we would just head back home, but no ... she said our adventure was only beginning. She told me to find Kingston on the map. In no time we were driving up King Street, circling round the thick limestone walls and red towers of the penitentiary. I remember staring up in horror at the bars and windows. But the best part of that day was yet to come. In fact, it's one of my fondest memories of my mother.

After checking into the motel, she insisted I choose a bed. Then we carefully laid out our dresses. Mom put on her makeup and I brushed my hair fifty-seven times. She let me powder my nose, reminding me how beautiful it was. Schnoz, a whatzer? A sneezer, Achoo, we rhymed. We had a little routine. I remember her kissing my nose eleven times for each glorious year of my existence.

Then we strolled down the main street to the restaurant. Mom asked the hostess for a quiet table for two, nodding at me. She ordered herself a glass of white wine and a Shirley Temple for me. It came garnished with two cherries and an orange slice on a tiny sword. I remember eating the fruit, and sticking the sword in my purse, alongside combs, pens and a notebook.

In a putting-on-the-Ritz tone, she suggested we peruse the dinner selections. As I looked at the children's list, she tapped the menu, saying, "The sky's the limit," and raised her glass to our journey!

I clinked my tall glass against hers. "To my mom." She stuck her tongue out at me. I made a face. We laughed uproariously, oblivious to the people at tables around us. She really made the evening special. I adored just being in her glow and soaking up her undivided attention.

As she sipped her wine, she asked if I was going to write about this weekend. I told her I'd already made notes while she was in the shower. That's when she gave me a small paper bag. Inside was a Shaeffer fountain pen and a box of blue and black ink cartridges.

"One day you'll be our Lois Lane—a writer has to have good pens," my mother said.

I asked, "Do you think maybe then I'll find my Superman?"

"You will," she said. "Now let's order the most decadent dessert ever!"

I paused in my storytelling and looked up at my three friends.

Kim laughed. "Sounds like your mom envisioned another up-and-coming Marian Engel."

Bear squeezed my hand. I felt my face turning twenty-five shades of crimson. I picked up the plates to load the dishwasher.

"I wish I had a mother like that," said Boyd. "The only place mine ever took me was to Sloan's for hot chocolate."

Twenty-Seven

All the way back to Toronto, I couldn't stop thinking about my mother. I wished I could be more like her. As we stopped at a roadside stand, I examined a basket of peaches, picking up one of the fruits and sniffing it. The scent transported me to the story of the day I was born.

It always began with a basket of Vineland peaches. My mother said during her pregnancy she had been continually ravenous and, on the day of my birth, the only food they had in the house was peaches. That is, except for a can of Smedley's peas. And who just eats a bowl of peas? Dad was working eighteen and a half hours a day at the restaurant and she had forgotten to ask him for the car to go to the grocery store. Lying prone on the couch, she devoured the juicy fruits one by one while reading Stephen King's book, *The Stand*. At this point in the tale, it was my cue to ask, "Why didn't you call me Frannie?" My mother said she had considered naming me after the main character in the book but she couldn't because she had a great-aunt Fran who terrified her. Years later, she gave me the hardcover version for my fourteenth birthday. As I read the heavy tome, I wondered what inspired her to read it at that time. It was a Stephen King novel of universal doom. But as I delved deeper into the narrative,

I understood the attraction and how she identified with the expectant heroine.

She told me when she reached the climax of the book, highlighted by an explosion, a sharp pain emanated through her midsection. She said it felt like someone had cinched a wide belt around her. She dropped the book to the floor. She was only eight months along. After the cramp subsided, she told herself it wasn't happening, only false labour. She leaned over and picked the book up where it had fallen onto a pile of peach pits, and once again began to read. Then another contraction hit. It took her a long time to wriggle off the sofa and get to her feet.

She phoned Dad, but no one answered. This is too soon, she kept telling herself. Stop baby, stop, she kept repeating. As usual, I didn't listen. She declared me stubborn from in utero. She weighed her options. She had no car to drive herself to the hospital. The drive-in theatre property was on the outer edge of town with the nearest neighbours at least a kilometre away. She called my dad again and let it ring and ring. He claims he didn't answer because he was stocking the freezer.

That's when the electricity went out. At first, she thought the light bulb on the reading lamp had burnt out but when she tried to switch on the bathroom light, she realized it was the power. She checked the fuse box as Dad had shown her, but none of them looked burnt. A pain hit again. She leaned against the wall and massaged her belly. When it subsided, she picked up the phone again. But it was dead.

I used to love to hear my mother say the next line, "I was in a real pickle."

And then I'd ask, "What happened next?"

"There was no one to help," she said. "You were my first and you were coming too soon. I racked my brain. I knew I couldn't walk into town. You would come for sure if I did that."

"And you didn't want me to be born on Ball's Flats Road—literally," I piped in.

"No, I didn't want to give you that legacy," said my mother, shaking her head. "I cursed myself for not phoning for an ambulance when the phone was still working. But then I remembered that your dad had bought a pile of fireworks for July first because..."

"He's a pyrotechnic junkie!" I would shout.

My mother loved telling this part of the story. "I dragged the box into the middle of the theatre parking lot. It was crammed with bottle rockets, missiles, and Roman candles. By the end, I was using my foot to shove it inch by inch across the yard. I needed to get it as far away from the house as possible."

"Weren't you scared that you'd blow us both up, Mom?" I would interject.

"A little bit. But I knew what I had to do. I lit a candle beside the open flap of the box and propelled my beach-ball body backwards as quickly as I could. I kept expecting to hear detonations as I scuttled away but nothing happened."

I always held my breath when my mother told this part of the story.

"I then waddled as fast as I could behind the house, squeezed up against the wall, holding my belly," she said.

"And then? Did it blow?" I would ask.

"I suspected the candle had blown out, but then I heard a small cracking sound. A rocket flew along the ground and into the woods. Then bang, bang, boom, one by one, three by three, the missiles exploded in every direction, most shooting up into the sky."

"It must have looked like a bomb went off!" I'd exclaim.

She nodded, beaming. "Apparently, you could see it from Gravenhurst. A fire truck, followed by three cruisers, roared down our road to see what was going on."

"Did they have their sirens on?" I'd ask.

"Yes, and lights flashing. They presumed it was teen-agers. Boy, were they stunned to see a roly-poly pregnant lady clutching an overnight bag, sitting on a lawn chair. They started to yell at me, but then noticed I was doubled over with a contraction. Instead, the captain radioed for an ambulance. The Muskoka hospital was not equipped to handle a prema-ture baby. So the doctors decided to send me to Toronto. As the attendants were shutting the doors, your dad jumped in. They raced down the highway while he rubbed my hand. By the time we arrived at the hospital he'd almost massaged the skin off my fingers. You were born at 6:47 PM at North York General face up..."

I would clap my hands at this point and shout my dad's line: "The size of a small bag of rice with a big fat smile." I loved how my father related everything to food. Even the legend of my birth.

Twenty-Eight

Back in Toronto, I continued to interview more women about body image. I discovered that, just like the story of one's birth, everyone had a chronicle about their body: an observation or a memory of the day they started feeling self-conscious or uncomfortable in their skin. I usually began the session with my set of questions but often abandoned them when I sensed the interview was heading in a more interesting direction.

Like my chat with Itsy. She had curled up in my cherished armchair, her feet barely touching the floor, while I had sprawled out on Aunt Binkie's couch with my notebook propped on my knees.

Itsy told me that people only see her size, not her face. Because her body looks like a ten-year-old girl, everyone assumes she is prepubescent. That first impression never lets them move on. During the interview, she covered her body with a blanket and asked, "How old do I look now?"

I was amazed. She looked like a woman in her early twenties, her correct age. I was so caught up in her itty-bitty feet that I wasn't seeing her face. "I notice you eat voraciously. How come you don't gain weight?"

"I have a fast metabolism, but my mother keeps warning me one day it will switch off and I'll turn into a watermelon." We laughed.

"What's your favourite body part?"

"My brain," she said, smiling. "I have a vivid imagination and can have fun anywhere."

I liked this girl more and more.

"What about your least favourite?"

"Body part?" she said, reflecting. "Honestly, I can't think of anything. To me, it all fits together. I can't really say I don't like my hips because they're joined to my legs." She looked curious. "You've done other interviews—what do other women say?"

I flipped back through my notepad and quoted the librarian who worked at the branch where I hung out. Her name was Dee Rousseau and she was over six feet tall. "My legs are too long," I read aloud. "Not proportionate to my body. My father is six-foot seven and his legs are shorter than mine. It's not like you can diet and your legs will get shorter. They called me Lurch. I haven't felt right about my body since I was thirteen."

"Poor girl," said Itsy. "I'm lucky—I don't feel that way at all. And I always think it's funny when people obsess over my size. Humans like to label each other too much, such as me—*Tiny*."

It was at that instant I saw a movement in Itsy's pocket. At first, I thought it was a figment of my imagination but then saw a small nose with a set of whiskers poking out. Itsy pulled a white mouse out of her pocket and let it run up her arm to her shoulder.

We'd been together for over a day and I hadn't noticed it before. "Have you had that mouse with you all along?" I asked. I wasn't sure how I felt about a rodent scurrying around my apartment.

She held the animal in the palm of her hand. "This is Spike. Actually, Spike the fourth. You can touch him. He won't bite."

I tentatively put a finger out and he sniffed and then ran back up Itsy's arm.

"I didn't tell you about him because most people are squeamish."

I tried to stay calm and stop the impulse to jump up on the couch. I looked around for Ziska, wondering why the dog hadn't noticed the little critter. "Does Marlin know about him?"

She laughed. "They met on the Ferris wheel. And it was love at first sight. Spike rode the whole way on his shoulder."

I looked down at the floor as if I might find mouse droppings everywhere.

"Don't worry—I clean up after him," she assured me. "Besides, he mostly stays in my pocket or perches on my shoulder." With that, the mouse traversed her body up and down like a running track before curling up on her left shoulder.

I had to admit he was rather sweet. I'd forgotten all about the interview. I picked up my fountain pen. "How would you categorize me?"

Itsy wiggled her nose, looking like her mouse. "You see that's exactly it. Why would I want to? You're more than the sum of your parts. Am I only a tiny woman with a mouse? No. Are you just a shapely woman with a great nose?"

I felt as if the elephant in the room had grown a thousand times bigger. Everything that had happened in the past few months landed on me. I burst into tears. I felt ugly. I was ugly. That's why Jake had left me.

Itsy knelt at my feet and stroked my hand. "See what I mean?"she said. "I'm so sorry. But you are so much more than those words. Your nose may be slightly large, but it is attractive. And you have beautiful blue eyes. I just don't notice your outer appearance. I see your inner warmth and kindness. Look how you welcomed me into your home without a moment's hesitation. I felt welcome from the moment I stepped through the door. Remember how I immediately fell asleep? I don't feel judged around you. And you have an amazing sense of humour, albeit overly self-deprecating sometimes." She wagged a finger at me. "Both you and Marlin are so much fun. I will never forget our day at the fair. All those rides, the candy floss."

Itsy had never eaten candy floss before and had bought two bags, getting the sticky pink sugar all over her face.

"You have to learn to accept yourself, Pen. We all get sucked into movie star magazine images of women. They are touched up photos — someone's ideal. They're not real."

I wondered how this twenty-one-year-old had gained so much wisdom. The more women I interviewed, the more I learned. Each had such diverse viewpoints. But a common thread for most — except for Itsy — was our deep lack of acceptance of who we were and what made us attractive to others.

After this discussion with Itsy, my next body image interview took place with June on the subway. We had started talking when I complimented her on her red shoes. She had smiled and told me they were her lucky pumps. They were Italian and she'd spent a week's pay for them. She was wearing them that day on her way to a weigh-in at Weight Watchers. She showed me a booklet that showed her progress. "I earned my ten-pound ribbon last week," she said with pride.

I told her about my article and asked if she would be interested in participating in an interview.

"What are you doing right now?" she asked, persuading me to attend her meeting. "Afterwards we could go for a coffee and talk."

She escorted me to a church basement where I was astounded to see women of every shape and size. June sat down to slip off her shoes before stepping on the scale. She let out a loud whoop—she'd lost another two pounds. At first during the meeting, I felt like I was back in kindergarten—the slender leader giving out stars and encouraging words. Then she told her own story of losing ninety-nine pounds. A murmur rippled through the room. She passed around a photo of her former state. "I ate because I was unhappy with my marriage," she explained. "Most of us are emotional eaters." The women all nodded. "Once I ate a whole gallon of maple ripple ice cream. After my divorce, I met my new husband-to-be at Baskin Robbins. I still like my ice cream."

I joined in the laughter.

June jumped up to introduce me as a guest, explaining that I was going to interview her about body image. Others clamoured to be included. I jotted down a list of names and telephone numbers. I had hit the jackpot.

After the meeting ended, we walked to a coffee shop and relaxed in comfortable wing chairs. June ordered a coffee with skim milk. She told me she had grown up in East York in a little wartime house. She was the third child of four. Her older brother's name was August, and her older sister, May. She and her sister were then called June and April, despite both of their birthdays were being in February. She shrugged her shoulders. "My mother insisted on continuing the tradition. My dad was an alcoholic and my mother eked out a living by re-boxing returned goods at the Max Factor plant." June couldn't remember when the fridge was ever full; every meal seemed to be plucked out of nowhere. A can of tuna, a box of macaroni, and a can of peas made a casserole that had to feed six mouths. "You had to grab fast or there'd be nothing left," she said.

"My Grade Two teacher somehow knew I came to school without breakfast," June continued, her voice shaky. "I loved Mrs. Dixon. She never made it obvious but would slip a granola bar or a banana into my desk." She stared into her coffee cup as if she could see the scene playing out.

I felt my eyes start welling up with tears as she told me her story.

"I was skeleton-thin as a teenager," June explained. "But not because I was throwing up or not choosing to eat—there was simply not enough to eat. As soon as I could, I got a job working at a fast food restaurant." She hesitated, and hung her head. "I used to sneak the leftovers on the trays, filching french fries or half-eaten burgers whenever I could. I was astounded that people would leave so much food on their plate. I was always hungry." She sipped her coffee and then plunked the mug on the table. "When I graduated high school and found a full-time job, I moved into my own basement apartment and instead of furniture or clothes, I bought food. Bags of groceries, wheeling them home in a wire cart. The only furniture I owned was an old couch I found at the Salvation Army and a black-and-white television my older brother handed down to me. I didn't even have a table or a bed. I ate and ate and ate, sitting in front of the television. Bowls of chips, heaps of spaghetti, tons of sticky buns. I craved carbs."

All this talking about food was making me hungry. I yawned. "I'm so sorry—I'm keeping you far too long," apologized June.

"No, no! It's just that I had lunch at eleven thirty," I said, glancing at my watch. "It's almost seven and I'm afraid I need to let Ziska out. She's my dog."

June's face spread into a wide smile. "This is the first time in my life that I have forgotten about dinner. Why don't we get your dog and go to Lick's Burgers? It's just down the street and we can eat outside. I can have a salad and a veggie burger and not go over on my points."

"Sounds good," I said.

Ziska wagged her short tail, eager to see me. We ran downstairs to the street. June raved at how cute she was, asking to hold the leash.

I ate my one hundred percent beef burger, breaking off a hunk of meat for Ziska.

June munched on her salad and continued her story. "I used to believe it was okay. My excuse was—some women buy make-up or clothes, while my passion was to keep a full pantry. I had rented my apartment on the basis of how big the refrigerator was."

She took a sip of water. I took out my notebook and began to write.

"I became obsessed," June said. "I didn't feel okay unless the cupboards were jam packed." She spoke with her hands as she talked, waving them in the air. "I applied for a credit card—I couldn't believe the bank approved me. I started taking out cash advances and buying food on my credit card.

Before I knew it, I had hit my limit and I could only afford to make minimum payments. Instead of dealing with it, I ate more."

I stopped taking furious notes, and just listened. "Then I met a man," June said. "He was one of the clients from the insurance office I worked for. He was a born-again Christian and told me that if I believed in Jesus Christ and accepted him as my saviour, the weight would melt off. I started dating him and I tried to stop eating. I prayed but nothing happened. In fact, I became so stressed, I put on twenty more pounds. He told me Jesus believed in handcuffs, too. It was then I kicked him out. But I had squandered a whole year with this drip."

I thought of the six years I had spent with Jake.

"When I told him to get lost, he had the audacity to call me a pig," she said, wincing. "It wasn't until that moment that I saw him for what he was. Two months later, I met Frank. It was then I realized what I had been missing in a relationship. Respect and acceptance."

"How did you meet Frank?" I asked.

June giggled. "He sold me these shoes. He's the nicest man. He loves well-rounded ladies, and he doesn't care if I lose an ounce." She picked at the bun on her veggie burger. "You know, it's funny. Since I met him, food isn't quite as appealing as before."

Twenty-Nine

I took a bite of my now cold burger, shoving it to one side. Had Jake ever respected or loved me? I thought about how he had refused to go to his department Christmas party. From time to time it had flashed through my mind that he looked embarrassed to be seen with me.

When we picked out movies at the video store, I let him choose. Otherwise he'd make a big scene about refusing to watch chick flicks. Unless it was an action picture, he wasn't interested. How many of those did I sit through while itching to sneak away to read a book? He disparaged fantasy movies like the *Lord of the Rings* trilogy. As if *Die Hard* was realistic! I realized that I was the one always compromising — it was all about Jake.

Walking home down Pape Avenue with Ziska prancing at my side, all I could think of was a glass of wine. I needed comfort and the numbness it would bring. I knocked on Bear's door, but no one answered. I stood in the dark hallway, feeling lost.

I opened my apartment door and turned on the radio. The haunting song, *Eleanor*, by the Montreal group Low Millions, was playing. Jake would have called the track rubbish. But I didn't care. The sad lyrics of the break-up song soothed my soul. It was good to know someone else out there was flailing about in misery.

Before Jake ran off, I knew deep down that he had changed, but I continued to convince myself I was fortunate to have him. I ignored his mood swings and how irrational he'd become. I hid it from my family and his, especially the obsession with his body. It was as if his muscles had snapped along with his psyche. Near the end, I was careful to ease into conversations, testing the waters, not wanting to stir anything up. Why had I put blinders on? Why was I chasing after him? Did I really want him back? How had I become so messed up? My rational self told me to get out, but some inner voice couldn't let him go.

I pressed my hands to my temples. The last time we made love was on a Wednesday. No surprise there. We had settled into timeslots right after his weekly session with his personal trainer. God forbid if we moved it to Monday. He planned sex both time-wise and how he desired to play it out. First, I must do X followed by Y. We did it in the dark. He did not kiss me anymore. He scarcely touched me. I touched him. He'd show me with gestures what he wanted. Thinking about it now made me nauseous. I had believed that my role and satisfaction lay in satisfying him.

Our physical attraction hadn't started this way. On our second date, he'd kissed me so passionately that I felt unravelled. We had parked in his mother's car on a cottage laneway, miles from town. Once his lips hit mine, we couldn't stop. It was hours of touching. I let him undo my bra. He stroked my back, and slowly we explored each other's skin.

We didn't go all the way that night. That happened three days later when we skipped math class. We snuck into my empty house and fell into my single bed between the cool slippery sheets. I unbuttoned my shirt. Showing off my new black bra. I had unzipped his pants and touched him. He sighed. It was like a game of chess. Silence. His move, followed by mine, counter move, zig-zag. Silence, communication by touch. Sensing we had gone too far, backing up. Hot, hotter, stop. I felt this wonderful buildup, this wanton need to let anything happen. I was wet and satiated as we mutely slipped back into our jeans.

The dam was opened. We would do it in the middle of the forest, using his jean jacket as a blanket. Or on the workbench in his grandfather's garage. We even snuck into Kim's boathouse and did it in a hammock—that was tricky. Yet lately what had it become? A boring, unfulfilling routine.

The very last time we had sex, he had hurt me. Not just the outer me, but the inner me and I hadn't protested. Now I loathed myself for it, despising him for having made me feel this way. On top of it all, he had been unreasonable and mean-spirited. "You could act a little more enthusiastic," he had said spitefully as he pulled up his boxer shorts. Then, unbelievably, I had immediately apologized as he dressed and left.

Once again, I chalked his behaviour up to a recently declined promotion. His manager had told him he needed to gain experience and handle himself more professionally. He responded to this criticism like a three-year-old. His face turned purple. "I want to smash his face," he screamed, pounding his hand through his front closet door. The lumber splintered. Raging, he tried to free his bleeding knuckles from the shards of wood.

Afterwards he apologized profusely. "I saw red," he kept saying. He lied to his mother about the broken door, telling her he had tripped over a pair of shoes in the hallway.

Thirty

The Low Millions song ended. I sat paralyzed for a few moments. Slowly, I got to my feet, and drifted down the stairs in a trance. Seven blocks later, I realized that I had no keys, no purse — my door was unlocked, with Ziska left sleeping on the couch. I stopped in my tracks and leaned against a streetlight.

A car barrelled past me and braked to a stop halfway up the block. It was a dark, boat-sized '80s sedan, idling noisily. No one got out of the car. I looked around but all the houses on the street were dark. The car jammed in reverse. I changed direction, walking fast, turning into an alley, my feet feeling heavy as cement blocks. Someone yelled. Behind me, the car swung its headlights like searchlights into the lane. Before they could see me, I propelled my body like a high jumper over a rickety fence, dropping with a thud into a garden.

I froze, holding my breath as the car rumbled by. When I could no longer hear the engine, I stood up, gasping for air. What the hell was I doing wandering the streets in the middle of the night? I realized I might have overreacted to the car. Too many horror movies watched at the Muskoka drive-in — my imagination on warp speed.

I slowly started limping home. After what seemed like hours, I spotted my apartment building. As I prepared to hobble across the street, a couple staggered down the sidewalk on the opposite side of the street. I concealed myself in the shadows of a hedge.

"When are you going to tell him?" asked a familiar voice.

Giselle snickered, grabbing Lucas's shoulder, swaying on her high heels. "Soon," she said. "First I need a little favour from the big old Bear."

"Do you think he'll kick me out?" Lucas said.

Giselle stopped, hands on her hips. "Ya' think? I'm sure he'll be pleased as punch to find we've been screwing right under his nose."

I put my hand over my mouth. How can they be so callous? It's one thing for a relationship to languish and end, but to find your lover in the arms of your roommate?

Lucas put his hand up under her skirt, kissing her hungrily. I stood on one foot and then the other. Were these two ever going to go inside? Lucas started to unbuckle his pants. Giselle grabbed his hand, opened the door and drew him inside. I waited, counting off three minutes, and then scooted across the street. I slowly pushed the door open — the lobby was deserted and I quietly slipped upstairs.

I stripped off my soiled clothes, turned the shower on and glanced at my image in the mirror. My midnight escapade had left no new blemishes on my face, but my hip ached where I had hit the ground. I was sure it would be black and blue in the morning.

I crawled into bed, wishing there was an on-and-off switch for my brain.

Bear's girlfriend was about to dump him and run off with his friend. I envisioned us both lying on my carpet listening and commiserating to the Low Millions *Ex-Girlfriends* album.

Then I recalled my recent interview with Giselle for the article. Bear had compelled me to include her, saying her experiences would be perfect grist for the mill. But I didn't feel comfortable. For some reason, she'd been too eager to co-operate. Maybe she thought she'd be photographed for the article and be in a magazine. Who knows? She dominated the interview before I even started.

"I hear you want to know about women and body image. I've never worried one iota about mine," she began, smoothing her skirt and posing like a diva.

I had sat in the wing chair, creating distance from where she postured on my couch. Clearing my throat, I asked my first question.

She interrupted. "I was thirteen," she said. "A boy moved next door. My father was long gone, it was just me, my mother and my older brother living in our house. They both worked so I had a lot of time to myself. Whenever I left the house I could see this boy watching me, his eyes zeroing in on my legs." She stroked her calf, smiling. "I loved to taunt the kid. I dropped my school books so I'd have to bend over and..."

I interjected. "And the boy was how old?"

She drew a manicured finger along her chin. "Maybe nine."

She then slid a foot in and out of her sandal. "Cute, but naïve as hell. One day I waited for him to catch up with me on my way home from school. I could tell he was keen to talk to me. He eyed me up and down, sneaking a peek down my blouse. I told him if he wanted to be my pal he'd have to pass a test."

How does a thirteen-year-old girl get to be so calculating, I wondered?

She continued. "I told him to climb a tree and when he was about ten feet up, I asked him to jump to the ground. He did it, no hesitation." She laughed. "No arguments, he'd do anything I asked. Carry my books. Do my chores. One day I told him the ultimate challenge would come that Saturday and if he did that he'd earn a very special prize. You should have seen the look on his face. I thought the poor baby was going to wet his pants."

A note of disdain slipped into my voice as I asked, "What does this have to do with…?"

"We'll get to that," she explained, clasping her hands behind her neck. She seemed to be enjoying this — she was inordinately calm, even smug. "I told him to meet me on Queen Street at ten. I arrived late. I knew he'd be there. We walked down to a store and along the way I described his mission — to steal me a pair of pantyhose. And they had to be black. He didn't flinch. He slipped into a store and was out within a minute, the loot tucked in his jeans. We ran all the way home." She giggled. "I decided to stretch out his reward. I grabbed the package and swung it in front of his face. I told him to meet me Sunday in the shed between our yards. I knew my mom would be at church and my brother would be passed out from drinking the night before. I gave him his reward. I can still see his face when he opened the shed door to see me wearing the pantyhose and a miniskirt."

A shiver had run up my spine. When I was the same age, I was riding my bike into town and reading Agatha Christie mysteries. Playing some erotic cat and mouse game with a Grade Four boy would never have crossed my mind. How could Bear be attracted to this woman?

"We met in the shed every day after school for a week," Giselle gloated. "Each day I'd have a new test. One day I asked him to pull his pants down. And he did!"

I'd had enough. "Excuse me. Why are you telling me this story?"

She put her hands on her hips. "Because it was the most exhilarating time of my life. I had planned on letting him touch the hosiery, but then he got grounded for stealing a chocolate bar. A few weeks later, he moved away."

I wasn't sure what to say next. Acting on remote, I began "Have you ever been on a diet and if so..."

"What a boring question," she said, yawning. "This interview is a drag." And with that, she swung her feet to the floor and pranced out of the room.

I couldn't get the scene out of my head. I rolled over in bed. And now she was two-timing Bear, I agonized. I was sure Bear had never heard the story about the nine-year-old boy.

Thirty-One

When I awoke, I found a note from Bear stuck to my door: *Don't forget Friday Night. Hint: Bring olives.* How was I going to face him, knowing about Giselle and Lucas? And more so, now knowing what she was capable of. I ripped the Post-It off the door, almost running smack into Lucas. He dashed past me in his work uniform, oblivious.

When I returned from work and mounted the last stair, I noticed the door to Bear's apartment was open. He waved at me from the kitchen where he was drying glasses with a tea towel, a fedora perched on his head. The man certainly knew how to make a simple cocktail into an event. I placed the jar on the counter. He plopped in three olives and handed me an oversized martini glass.

"Friday night," he said. We clinked our chilled glasses together before sipping. "Giselle's at her cousin's and Lucas had to work overtime. Tonight, it's just us girls." He laughed.

I wondered what shady bar those two were undoubtedly huddled at. I forced myself to keep my mouth shut while the warning "Wake up and smell the roses!" screamed inside my head.

"Hey Pen, you're quiet tonight," he said. "What's on your mind?" But he didn't wait for me to answer. "Let's tip back a few of these libations and mosey on down the street to a new restaurant I've heard about. How about appetizers? I have a hankering for some of that flaming cheese. What do the Greeks call it?"

I shook my head.

The martini was not sitting well and I suddenly felt exhausted. It was most likely from the previous night's misadventure. Not to mention my newfound knowledge of Giselle and Lucas. I set the glass down on the counter. "Sorry, but I have to pass. I'm feeling a bit queasy."

Bear escorted me back to my apartment and insisted on tucking me into bed, setting a bowl on the floor beside me, just in case. He carried a snoring Ziska in to cuddle with me and switched off the light, leaving me to my thoughts. As I lay there, I thought about relationships. Happy relationships. And my mind drifted back to a day on Lake Rosseau with Mom and Dad.

Thirty-Two

I remember it was a day in June. Dad was shaving, preparing to leave for the restaurant. He never took time off; the food business was eternally shaky and he was afraid to close down even for a day.

I was lying in bed when I heard the tap shut off in the bathroom. I rolled over, falling back asleep. Exams were over and I had the whole summer off, a virtual eternity. Suddenly, Dad was banging on my door open, his face covered in shaving cream.

"Where are your big black markers?" he asked. "I need you to make me a sign."

I sat bolt upright, the sheets clutched to my chest.

Marlin stumbled by my door, still half asleep.

"Find your bathing suits," bellowed our father, scraping the remaining shaving cream off with his razor.

It was the year my brother was in Grade Seven and he still had more than a week of classes left. "You mean I don't have to go to school?" said Marlin.

Dad nodded and my brother suddenly came to life.

Dad handed me a piece of cardboard. "Write: *Restaurant closed for the day. Gone Fishing. See you Thursday.*"

I looked up at him. "Are you sure?"

He had tickled me under the arm. "Your father has declared today: Gone Fishing Day. Now go unearth my tackle box and grab some beach towels."

Mom poked her head around the corner. "You've what?"

"I'm taking the day off and we're all going out on Lake Rosseau," Dad announced. "Don't bother to pack food — we'll grab sandwich fixings from the restaurant when we post the sign. Hurry up," he hollered, shooing us into our rooms. "I have to call Bruce and Jeannie and give them the day off too."

Within an hour, we were lakeside. Dad reversed the car and trailer down to the boat launch and pulled on the emergency brake. He released the cedar strip boat into the water. I waded in, flinging the cooler and life jackets under the bow. He then helped Mom into the boat. I passed him the fishing rods and Marlin lugged the tackle box from the trunk. The motor started with one pull. "Trusty little beast," said our dad to no one in particular.

We puttered down the Indian River and into the main lake. I loved the feeling of the water spraying my face as the boat planed out. I knew where he was headed. He always tried his fishing luck in Brackenrig Bay, just past the tiny town island.

Dad wasn't like Mom — he didn't normally talk much about the past. He'd ask us about our schoolwork or tell amusing anecdotes about the restaurant from time to time. As we drifted, he had his line in the water but I could tell he was concentrating on something more than catching fish.

"We weren't going to have a honeymoon," he began. Marlin and I locked eyes. We'd never heard this story before. Mom said nothing, not one word.

"We had no money for frivolities," he said. "For two years, I'd saved all of my tips, hoping it would be enough for a down payment on a townhouse on Warden Avenue. We got married at Toronto City Hall and then went to my cousin Nick's restaurant with our closest friends to celebrate. After dinner, Helen—she was the one who stood up for your mother—gave us a present. We opened up a small box. Inside was a key and a map. Helen told us it was her family's cottage in Muskoka but assured us no one would be up for the season yet. We couldn't believe our good fortune. A real honeymoon! We were giddy with the prospect but then I realized we had no car.

"Without blinking," Dad shared, "Nick tossed me the keys to his Austin 1800. We were speechless. Everyone was so generous. Nick had already supplied the drinks and food for our reception, and now he was loaning us his beloved car with a trunk full of food."

I remember seeing tears well up in Mom's eyes as the boat rocked back and forth.

My father then shifted in his seat and cleared his throat. "Next day, we woke at dawn and in no time hit the outskirts of Toronto. To see these fields rolling out to the horizon was a thrill. We kept looking at the map to check our progress. It was a winding highway out to Port. Your mother's face turned green every time we went around a corner driving through those immense rock cuts at Milford Bay. We stopped in Bracebridge to buy some fresh meat and milk."

"And a bottle of wine," our mom reminded him.

Laughing, he added, "If the highway was bad, the cottage road was like a roller coaster, dipping and weaving around rocks and trees, narrowing down to one lane. Soon a little white sign with the name Woods directed us up a vertical driveway."

Dad still hadn't hooked a fish — I was hanging on to his every word.

"Through the trees, you could see down to a lake," he said excitedly. "I opened the door to the cottage. Your mother ran inside first and dropped her suitcase. A wide picture window overlooked the lake a hundred feet below."

"We thought we'd died and gone to heaven," Mom laughed.

Dad continued. "We found a path and followed it down a hill past a colossal teardrop-shaped rock and a flight of stairs, lined with white railings. At the bottom of the second staircase we came upon a kiddie swimming area with a dock that protected it from the lake. A red slide stood on the sandy bottom. To the right was a granite patio. We wandered to the edge. I bounced on the diving board and peered into deep water. Turning, I caught hold of an immense boathouse with a flat roof covered in patio furniture. Your mother grabbed my arm. 'We must be dreaming,' she said.

"Suddenly, we heard a phone ringing," Dad said. "It was coming from the boathouse so we opened the door. The phone was on a large desk made out of a giant slice of a tree trunk. Your mother pushed past me and picked up the receiver. It was Helen welcoming us and suggesting we use the small cedar strip boat and visit Port Carling. She said we were standing in her grandfather's den — his cottage was actually on the other side of the boathouse.

"The property was more like a resort than a cottage, except we were the only guests. We knocked on Helen's grandparents' door. No one was there. We wandered down a magnificent stone staircase, discovering a man-made river and a waterfall with a small logging mill and gnomes around the lily pond."

Dad continued, "We took another rocky path that led to the main boathouse, filled with tire tubes, lifejackets, fishing gear, and tools. There were three boat slips, and in one, a mahogany cigar-shaped boat caught my eye. It was mid-afternoon and as hot as Hades. The lake was looking pretty inviting. Since it was a long walk uphill to get our bathing suits, your mom undressed and dove into the water. I couldn't get my clothes off fast enough."

I sat up and stared at Dad. I couldn't imagine him skinny dipping. He was so Old School.

"The water felt like silk," he said. "We swam out to a raft and back, grabbed our clothes and dashed up the hill. As we did, we ran smack into a man coming down the hill," he added, chuckling.

"Bare-naked?" I remember Marlin asking. And my mother had nodded, tossing her head back with laughter.

"It was just the caretaker," Dad explained as he reached across the boat and kissed my mother on the nose. "The place was paradise—canoeing, boating to buy steak and wine, swimming, reading in the hammocks eating cheese and grapes. But the boathouse was my favourite spot," he reminisced. "The smell reminded me of my boyhood home in Greece. I loved that mahogany boat and one afternoon, when your mother was napping, I jumped into the boat and opened the engine doors.

"'Want to take it for a spin?' asked a voice.

"I almost hit my head on the door. I looked up to see a white-haired older man wearing a Hawaiian shirt and sporting a Panama hat.

"'I'm Helen's grandfather,' he said, shaking my hand. He stepped into the driver's seat and motioned for me to cast off. After barrelling into the bay, I couldn't believe it when he slipped out of the seat and signalled for me to take the wheel. Your mom would have loved it!"

Dad now turned our boat through the narrow waterway between the island with the miniature village and the mainland. He sped up and the little Johnson motor roared as we passed a boathouse with three slips. Then we saw it—a window peeking through in the trees. The cottage. He slowed down.

"Dad!" I called out, pointing as we passed the diving board and a raft where I could see a sandy beach blocked off by the dock and a red slide partially immersed in the water. "This is it—the place where you and Mom shared your idyllic honeymoon!"

Mom finally broke her rare silence and described the next chapter in their life. "You can see why we fell in love with this part of the province. We weren't sure what we should do but by the end of that week we decided not to buy the house in Scarborough. A luxurious cottage is not real life. We knew we would have to find jobs. On our way home, we stopped in town. Wandering down the street, we came upon a faded *For Rent* sign in a storefront. Through the dusty window, your father saw a counter and stools and a milkshake machine. In that moment, our destiny was clear. We could use our down payment money to start up the business. But what would we do for a house?"

"I know what happened then," said Marlin, splashing his feet in the water.

Mom leaned her head against Dad's shoulder. "Obviously, we couldn't afford anything on the lake or in town. But our real estate woman called us and told us about an unusual property that had just come on the market."

"The drive-in theatre!" Marlin and I yelled in unison.

"*Our* paradise," she smiled lovingly.

Thirty-Three

I was never able to persuade my father to take a *Gone Fishing* day again. After my mother died, he became married to the restaurant, practically living there. Like a kid who wished for her divorced parents to reunite, I ached for my father to recover. I knew my prayers would never bring my mother back but I searched for a woman for my father to fall in love with. Two years after her death, I suggested he ask Jeannie out. He told me to mind my business. "No one will replace your mother," he murmured, slapping the spatula down on the grill.

The more morose my father had become, the more my brother followed suit. Despite how loud and boisterous he was with me, he walked around like a ghost in high school, talking to no one. I asked him to join in activities with Kim and me, but he always bowed out at the last minute, swearing he had an essay to write or giving some other inane excuse. If my connection with my mother was tight, my brother's had been like contact cement. I worried that her sudden death had unglued him. At her wake, he had fled into the forest behind the house and he didn't come back until dawn the next day. I fretted over him, but it was actually Jake who had snapped him out of it.

Not that Jake and Marlin were friends. I realized this as I watched the new relationship with my brother and Bear. Marlin called Bear at least once a week. They were already planning a guitar jam session with some of my brother's buddies. My brother would never have called Jake.

Just then, Marlin phoned to tell me that Dad was giving Itsy more responsibilities, counting stock and balancing the cash on Jeannie's nights off. We both knew this was a significant stretch for our father. Normally he trusted no one except Jeannie. During the call, I caught Marlin off guard and asked him exactly how Jake had managed to help him move on after Mom's funeral.

He exhaled deeply into the phone. "You don't want to hear this."

"Yes, I do. I've been thinking about it. Maybe it will help me understand him."

"It's not a discussion to have on the phone."

"C'mon. What happened?" I demanded.

He groaned. "When you were working at the restaurant one night, Jake drove out to the house." He stopped. His voice grew angry. "There's no point in talking about this now."

"What happened? Tell me."

There was a long silence—I thought the line had gone dead. But then he resumed speaking, his voice low. "Jake pushed me down on the ground, holding me down. He told me to get over it. My mother was gone and I should be a man and grow some balls. He said me if I didn't stop acting like a snivelling brat, he was going to beat the living shit out of me."

My legs felt weak. "Why didn't you tell me this before? Or at least Dad?"

"Do you think you would have believed me? In your eyes, he was a god. And did Dad need one more thing to worry about?"

Things were crashing into focus. There was my Jake, and then there was everyone else's Jake. I now remembered Kim having heart-to-heart talks with me about playing the field, not getting too serious. I had completely ignored her, thinking she was jealous because she didn't have a boyfriend at the time and didn't understand relationships. How could I have been so blind?

After I talked to Marlin, I dug out one of my old Moleskines. A few months ago, I had recorded the names of the products and powders Jake used in his protein shakes every morning. While Jake was in the shower, I had discovered them hidden on the shelf in his closet in an insulated lunch bag. I had ripped open the Velcro strip to find a clear bottle of liquid and needles. He found me examining an unlabelled bottle, snatching it from my hand. "Don't have a conniption," he had said, "Those are vitamins in liquid form." And I had brushed it off. Jake would never do anything to harm himself. I had forgotten about the incident, but now I turned on my laptop and entered the word: steroids.

I learned from Wikipedia that anabolic steroids had been developed to help victims of cancer and AIDS and were also used in sports to build up muscle mass and physique. However, they were controversial due to the unfair advantage they provided in competition as well as their adverse side effects. The downside was not pretty. I hit many sites on the subject and one key element kept surfacing. Mood swings. I shuddered. Over the past year and a half, Jake had doubled both his chest size and his tendency to go ballistic.

The last time we had visited his father and his new wife Beverly in North Bay, Jake had gone atomic. When she asked casually about his mother at dinner, he whipped the bread basket across the table.

"How do you think she's doing, you silly bitch? You stole her husband, you messed up her life." I felt like hiding under the table. I knew he hated his father, only visiting under duress, but where had this recent fury come from?

His father coolly asked him to pick up the bread and apologize. When he refused, his dad asked him to leave. There was a tussle between them and Jake put his father into a stranglehold.

Beverly was crying. I screamed, "Let him go."

I drove home that night with Jake ranting non-stop. By the time I pulled into his driveway, his temper had cooled and he admitted he'd gone overboard. We started to joke about it. He promised to call his dad to apologize. I doubt he ever did.

We used to hang out every weekend with Kim and Boyd, but that had been curtailed too. I had forgotten this. He moaned about being fed up with Boyd, as he only talked about house design. And how Kim was always needling him. I wondered if she knew about the steroids. Jake had told me my best friend was a spoiled rich kid who was manipulating me. He suggested I should be careful because Kim was talking behind my back.

Thirty-Four

I stood in a corridor at McMaster and boldly asked the next passer-by where I could find the physiotherapy labs. The university office had refused to disclose any information about students, quoting the privacy act. As I explored the campus, I envied students rushing from class to class. This part of Hamilton seemed so alien to the industrialized environment I'd visited before. I snuck into a lecture hall but I didn't see the fair-haired Ginger anywhere. Fearful of missing her, I stood at the door and studied each blonde's face as the class ended. No luck.

I approached the last straggler. "Do you know many of the women in the program?"

The student shook his head.

I made up a story of looking for a long-lost friend and inquired if he knew how I might find her.

He appeared interested in helping me out. "You know, there's a mixer tonight."

"A what?" I asked.

He pointed to a handbill stapled to the board outside the classroom: *Pub Night – Physiotherapy Students. Join us for "moving" conversation and "rehabilitating" drinks.* I shook the student's hand energetically. It was perfect. An electric shock ran down my back as I jotted down the information. I'd have to switch shifts with someone at work but I knew I had to attend. There was no doubt that Miss Ginger would be there, and very likely Jake.

I returned triumphantly to my apartment, banging on Bear's door. This was one mixer I didn't want to attend alone. I prayed that Giselle had waited a few more days before divulging her affair.

But Bear had news of his own. He was practically bouncing. "Giselle has an audition in Los Angeles. I'm lending her the money to fly out there for a few weeks."

I froze. "How much money?" I asked.

"Five thousand dollars," he said, beaming. "I knew if she was patient, something would open up for her." He showed me his bank passbook. "Look, I have exactly five thousand and eleven dollars and five cents in my savings account."

I bit my tongue. How typical of his wily girlfriend to take practically every cent he had. I shuddered just thinking of the night Giselle had told Lucas she had one more favour to ask of the old Bear.

"It's the start-up money for my business. But if it helps Giselle with her career, it can wait."

I had to say something. I couldn't let him be swindled out of his total savings. But just then, Lucas walked up the stairs carrying numerous liquor store boxes.

"Moving out?" asked Bear, jokingly.

His roommate's face reddened. "Very funny. I'm just cleaning out some junk to give to my kid brother."

Bear clapped Lucas on the back. "Good idea, your room is a fire hazard."

I felt my jaw freeze. I simply had to tell him now.

He turned to me. "I'll take you to Hamilton on one condition."

I nodded.

"It's my dad's birthday. My mother appealed to my better side and roped me into coming for dinner. It's on the way — we'll just pop in."

I agreed and left quickly, volunteering nothing about Giselle. It was true Ziska needed to do her business, but the words *coward, weak, selfish* echoed in my head. I hated to be the bearer of bad news but I couldn't meet Jake and his paramour without Bear to back me up. If I told him now, he might be too upset to take me. I promised myself that as soon as I found Jake, I'd spill the beans.

Thirty-Five

I wore my best outfit. Kim had made me a daisy-patterned skirt for my birthday, the hem a perfect length. I pulled on a lacy white camisole I'd found on sale at *The Bay*. I twisted a lock of hair to the side with a clip and I even dug out a lipstick. Hot red. I wiped the dust off my ruby sandals. I hoped they'd bring me as much luck as June's red pumps.

Bear raved that I was a vision. I reciprocated by calling him a sight to behold. He had gone to the barber shop; his hair was neatly cut and his beard trimmed. He wore jeans and a starched white shirt and real shoes in lieu of his usual old runners or Crocs. After slipping on his black blazer, he waited for me at the door, smelling like freshly laundered towels.

In one of our late-night chats, he had told me his parents lived in a small house by Lake Ontario. When we rolled into the circular driveway, passing two regal lion statues guarding the gates, I gasped, "This is what you call small?"

I was surprised when he rang the bell outside the impressive double oak front doors. Why not just walk in? His father answered, not a butler or a maid as I imagined. He gave a bone-crunching hug to his son and then to me.

Bear didn't resemble his father. His dad's lean body and bald head reminded me more of the actor Ed Harris. I started worrying about his poor mother's features.

I heard her before I saw her. "Is that Truman?" screeched an animated voice. She appeared at the top of a double staircase, dressed in a black cocktail dress. Her bright orange hair was flawlessly coiffed in waves around her face. She swung her hip up onto the oak banister, gliding down, making a perfect landing on two feet on the marble foyer floor. Without blinking an eye, she held out a manicured hand to greet me. "Giselle, I presume?"

"No, no. Giselle couldn't make it. This is my friend, Pen," said Bear, putting his arm around my shoulder. "And these are my parents, Vicky and Eric."

I stood speechless. His mother's unorthodox entrance was only exceeded by the discovery that his real name was Truman. If Bear thought my family and our living quarters were captivating, I was equally amused by his.

"What happened to Gina?" asked his father.

Bear cleared his throat. "Giselle," he corrected. "She had to visit her sick aunt."

How many relatives can one woman invent, I wondered. Yes, I would definitely tell him tonight about Giselle and her secret life of lies.

"I was at sixes and sevens all day," said his mother, grabbing my arm and leading me into an auditorium-size living room. Everything in the room was white; the thick rug, the couches, the wing chairs, tables, the roses in a huge crystal vase. The only splash of colour was the burnt orange cushions tossed on the couch. Even the brick fireplace had been painted snow white. "I was deliberating on the menu for tonight and nothing seemed quite right."

A gray-haired woman in an apron entered with a tray. My hand trembled as I reached for a goblet of red wine. The white surroundings made me nervous. I envisioned placing the glass down and missing the coffee table.

Bear declined a drink. "I'm driving. We have an engagement at McMaster after dinner."

"A party?" his father asked.

I crossed my legs, the wine glass tipping slightly. I managed to level it before a drop escaped.

Bear was evasive. "We're meeting up with a few friends of Pen's."

The conversation turned to Giselle's good fortune, the audition in the States. Bear didn't mention he was giving her money. It crossed my mind, as I regarded his parents' house, that maybe that his bank account wasn't much of an issue. Five thousand dollars to me was a fortune.

"How long have you two been friends?" asked Eric.

"Pen moved in this summer," said Bear, answering for me. "She's a journalist."

"What periodical do you work for?" inquired his mother. But before I could answer, a bell rang. Vicky jumped to her feet. "Strike while the iron is hot." I could see where Bear had inherited his bevy of clichés. His mother chatted non-stop as she led us into a dining room. "When I realized I couldn't decide on tonight's menu, I simply told Edie to surprise us. She's been cooking up a storm all afternoon."

I sat across from Bear, a set of silverware spread out in front of me like a tray of medical instruments. His parents were a kilometre away to the south and north. "I thought you had Dennis take out some of the table leaves," shouted Eric to his wife.

Vicky clicked her tongue. "It doesn't seem very intimate, does it?"

The woman who had served the wine pushed open a door, laden with bowls of soup.

Vicky waved her hands. "Oh Edie, it smells divine. I hate to ask, but could you take it back to the breakfast room?" The cook's eyes flashed with exasperation. I imagined his mother's over-the-top enthusiasm and reversing requests might become grating.

Eric held open the door and we followed the steaming soup to the rear of the house. My mouth was watering. We settled around a small, round table, the cook flying to the kitchen for cutlery and napkins. I dipped my bread into the creamy broth.

The main course was chicken pot pie. At first, I thought it rather ordinary for a birthday dinner, but that was before I sunk my fork into the chunks of breast meat with button mushrooms, a smooth, delicious sauce and puff pastry that melted in your mouth. If I had had more room, I would have asked for thirds.

Over dinner I sipped another glass of wine. I thought it might help build up my nerve for the next part of our junket. "Bear really saved me the day I moved in," I informed his parents, describing how he had helped lift the heavy furniture up four flights of stairs.

"Was the elevator not working?" asked his dad. "Truman has never invited us to his den."

"Oh, Eric," said his mother, "If he wasn't independent, you'd be complaining that he was bleeding you dry." She wiped her mouth with the cloth napkin and placed it on her lap. "We just miss our one and only son and wish we saw more of him."

Bear took this opportunity to pull a small box out of his pocket. It was wrapped in what looked like a Far Side cartoon, cut out of the newspaper. "Happy birthday," he said, handing it to his father.

Eric's face flushed. He opened the box. "Good God. It's a 1950 penny. A good luck birthday coin." It looked shiny, as if it had just been stamped at the mint. Eric shot from his chair to embrace and thank his son. "I'll add it to my collection." His eyes shone as he held it up to the light. Bear looked over at me and winked.

Suddenly the lights went dim. Edie stepped in with a tray containing four ramekins, a candle in each. Eric clapped his hands. "Crème Brûlée. My favourite!" He blew out the candles. I was full, but when I slipped my spoon into the crunchy brown top and cream below, it tasted otherworldly. I was hooked.

I enjoyed talking with Bear's parents so much that I almost forgot about Jake. I was accepting a second cup of coffee when Bear announced it time to go.

We made a promise to visit again soon.

"Maybe one day we'll be invited into Toronto," sighed Vicky, leaning against her son's shoulder.

"Come to my place any time," I offered, feeling a little tipsy.

As we headed back to the highway I sighed. "I would put your parents on my top ten list of..."

Bear interrupted. "Screwballs?"

I laughed. "You say that as if it's a bad thing."

In no time, I drifted off into a wine-soaked reverie. The next thing I knew, we had arrived on campus.

"Shall we do some sleuthing?" asked Bear.

I looked at him blankly, now wondering why I was so set on continuing this quest. Perhaps it was because of Jake's mother. Ann had called me anxiously the previous night. Even though she knew Jake was not in any danger, something seemed off-kilter to her.

"Did he tell you what happened the night before he left?" she had asked, sniffling.

I sat up. "What are you talking about?"

Her voice had cracked. "I used the last of the milk to make a cake. There wasn't enough for him to mix up one of his infernal drinks. He had a meltdown and called me a horrible mother. You would have thought I'd shot the dog, not run out of milk. How could he still be angry with me?"

Thirty-Six

Bear and I were at the door of the pub when his cell phone rang. I prayed it wasn't Giselle. He answered but immediately handed the phone over to me. It was Marlin, out of breath.

"I've being trying to reach you all night," he said. "There's two hundred dollars missing out of the till — Dad has accused Itsy."

"Have you recounted the money?"

"Dad went over it ten times. The cash is gone and only Dad, Jeannie and Itsy have access to it."

I tried to craft my sentence carefully. "Marlin, we don't know her very well."

"Damn it!" He yelled so loud, I had to pull the phone away from my ear. "She swears she didn't take it!"

"Okay, simmer down," I said. Bear looked at me quizzically. I placed the palm of my hand over the receiver. "There's money missing at the restaurant and Dad thinks it was Itsy." I placed the phone back to my ear.

"I've never seen him so angry. Something is up," said Marlin.

I explained to my brother that Bear and I were at a noisy bar and promised to call him back when I returned home. I neglected to tell him that I was on Jake's trail.

When we stepped inside the pub, a din of voices greeted us. The music was scarcely audible under the roar. We pushed our way to the bar and Bear ordered two Pink Ladies.

I raised my eyebrows. "I like to mess with bartenders' heads, see if they're up on their cocktails."

The girl looked exasperated but scurried away, probably to find a bar recipe book. Her forte was obviously drawing beer and uncorking wine bottles.

We stood around for half an hour, awkwardly trying to blend in. There were so many people, it was hard to survey the room.

Then I heard him. It was Jake's fake laugh—I could recognize it anywhere. My drink soured in my mouth. I put it down on the nearby bar and grabbed Bear's hand, squeezing into the crush of students.

I felt my senses heighten. I couldn't make out his words, but slowly I moved towards his voice. Then I saw him. His back was turned towards me and I could see his bulging neck. A tight short-sleeved golf shirt accentuated every muscle. A group of people stood around him—he had his arm wrapped around a brunette. It almost seemed like he was holding her prisoner. Could this be the same girl from the Ex? Where was the blonde? I edged closer. I could smell him now, the pungent cheap cologne he thought was so beguiling. His voice droned on and on. To my surprise, Bear slipped by me and broke into the ring of listeners. Jake glanced in his direction and then away dismissively.

I watched Bear, nodding as Jake continued his story. Unable to decipher Jake's words, I inched forward, standing right behind him. Bear made a motion with his hand, miming shooting himself in the temple. I studied the brunette's profile, examining her nose. Believe it or not, it was Ginger. She had dyed her hair and, without the flashy make-up, she looked quite unremarkable.

I felt my fists clenching. I had finally hunted him down. I had rehearsed lunging at him, shoving him to the floor and screaming abuse. But I took a step back. The whole situation and our relationship now seemed false and meaningless. I had nothing to say to him. I didn't know this person anymore. In fact, I wondered if I ever had. I just wanted to distance myself from this place and from him forever. I signalled to Bear and pointed to the door.

Jake's voice grew louder. "She saved me," he said, pulling the giggling Ginger closer, "from a fate worse than death. I was stuck in a one-horse town, practically engaged to Princess Fiona. Shrek can have that dog."

Slowly Bear lifted his fist. I looked helplessly at Jake's jaw. I stepped further back. Bear looked like he was going to follow, but instead stumbled forward wildly, spilling a full pink cocktail on Jake's white shirt and Ginger. "So very sorry," he said, pushing by.

Jake swung around, his face contorted with anger. And then he saw me and froze.

His new girlfriend wiped the collateral damage from her face and turned around too. "Oh, my Lord," she said, smirking. "It's her."

"Is that the old girlfriend?" one of Ginger's classmates asked Jake.

Ignoring the question, Jake grabbed my shoulders and started shaking me. "I can't believe you would stoop this low."

With that, Bear wrenched Jake's arm around his back and quickly immobilized him. "Apologize to her," he spat.

"Who the hell are you?" asked Jake, panting heavily, and struggling to free himself from Bear's arms.

"I know all about you!" I blurted out. "Your secrets and addictions. If you possess one drop of human decency, you'll call your mother," I uttered between clenched teeth.

Bear slowly released his grip and shoved him roughly aside.

Instinctively, I started to run from the pub. I didn't stop until I found myself in the middle of a distant parking lot and I heard Bear yelling. "Stop, wait up!"

I slowed down. He caught up and put his cell phone into my hand. "Call Marlin. Your dad's been rushed to hospital."

My legs bowed, turning to jelly. Bear grabbed my arm. The first thing that flashed through my mind was, please ... not my mother all over again. Not now. I can't take it. Losing one parent was enough. My unlucky streak was closing in on me. I couldn't catch my breath.

Thirty-Seven

Bear drove to Toronto and rushed upstairs to retrieve Ziska. We then headed north. I sat bolt upright, unmoving, all the way to Bracebridge, Ziska curled up silently on my lap. When we pulled into the emergency room driveway, I sprinted inside and ran smack into Kim. I didn't like the look on her face. It was not a good news expression. It was the how-do-I-tell-you-this look. She pushed me into a stairwell.

"Don't," I begged, covering my ears. "Please, don't."

Kim shook me. "Settle down. He's still in surgery. Your dad's gall bladder burst and ruptured his bowel. It's a bit dicey."

"Is he going to live?"

Kim put her arm over my shoulder. "I'll take you to the surgical waiting room where Marlin is."

Bear looked lost standing in the middle of the emergency corridor. Kim took him by the hand and led us up the stairs. My brother and Itsy were crouched on chairs in a dark room called the Quiet Room. Marlin jumped to his feet when he saw me. We clung to one another for what seemed like an eternity.

Kim left the room, promising to get us a progress report. She was gone for a long time. That's when I started to pace.

"Dad found the money," Marlin said quietly.

I halted mid-route to a chair. "Where was it?"

"In his pocket. When he had one of the attacks, he forgot about taking cash out of the till to pay the dairy order. Apparently, he has been in pain for weeks, refusing to tell anybody. He thought it was his back acting up again."

Itsy had not said a word. Her head was down.

"Are you okay?" I asked her. My dad had accused her of theft.

She looked up and took my hand into hers. "Me? Of course. I knew your dad was just upset."

Marlin checked his watch for the umpteenth time. "He's been in surgery a long time."

Boyd poked his nose in the door. "May I come in?" He sat down. For a few minutes no one talked. He looked like he was searching for the right thing to say. "Your dad was such a good guy."

I cut him off. "Was? Do you know something we don't?"

"No, no," he said, shaking his head. "Sorry. What I meant is, he *is* a good guy!"

A doctor in scrubs entered the room followed by Kim, wearing her professional facade. I could not read their faces. But then I saw her wink.

"He's holding his own," said the doctor. "It was complicated, but he's in recovery now."

"Were there any other organs affected?" asked Bear.

"The gall bladder ruptured into the bowel, the liver and the bile ducts so it took longer than normal to repair all the injuries. We had to be particularly careful not to further damage the bowel."

"When can we see him?" asked Marlin.

"He should be coming out of anaesthesia shortly," said the surgeon, pulling off his cap. "I'll have the nurse come and find you when he's awake. But only the immediate family can see him."

When Dad was moved into the intensive care unit, Marlin and I were allowed into his room but he was too groggy to speak. Kim insisted we leave and get some sleep. She would call when he was lucid.

I returned at dawn. It was difficult to see my father lying helpless in that hospital bed, connected to a myriad of hoses, cables and tubes. A small screen above the bed showed three blipping coloured lines and a variety of digital read-outs. My father's eyes were closed, his face pale. I studied the screen, having absolutely no idea what I should be looking for.

Then I heard my dad's weak voice. "Am I alive?"

I touched his hand, careful to avoid the needle poking out above his knuckles. "You scared us half to death. Why didn't you go to the doctor? Why didn't you tell Marlin you were in pain?"

He frowned. "I didn't want to worry anyone."

There was no point in reprimanding him.

"I like that Bear," he mumbled.

"The guy that drove me here at breakneck speed last night?" I asked, smiling.

He grinned. "Actually, this morphine is quite nice," he said, now lounging back on the pillows.

Marlin opened the sliding glass door.

My father struggled to sit up. "Where's Itsy? I have to apologize."

Marlin pulled a chair up beside the bed. "Relax. It's all water under the bridge. She's just happy you're okay."

"She didn't leave?" My father's voice sounded plaintive.

Marlin shook his head. "Right now, she and Bear are covering the breakfast rush."

For a moment, a look of panic flashed across my dad's face. Then he sighed. "You know, I completely forgot about the restaurant."

Thirty-Eight

The next morning, I called Toronto and quit my job at Honest Ed's. For the time being, I was needed in Bracebridge to help keep the family business running. Soon I'd return home and find another job. It felt strange, but for the first time in months, I felt energized.

I drove back to the city in my old car to pick up some clothes and pay my bills. I packed a few bags and checked my phone messages. There was one from Ann, thanking me for finding Jake. He had obviously called her. I felt nothing. In fact, he had not crossed my mind since we received the call about my father. Jake had used me. I was simply a means to an end for him. He'd never loved me, and I realized that he had never said the words. I'd swallowed the whole illusion of romantic love — hook, line and sinker. I smiled to myself. That could be a Bear line.

I picked up my interview notebooks and crammed them into my backpack. I'd have time between shifts at the restaurant to complete the article before returning to Toronto. I zipped up my suitcase. Suddenly my stomach lurched. Giselle. I had planned to tell Bear about her and how she had bamboozled him into emptying his bank account, but I'd messed that up too. In the melee, I had completely forgotten.

What kind of a friend would do that? Now it was probably too late. Chances are Giselle had already left with money in hand.

I knocked on Bear's door. There was no answer. The day after helping in the restaurant, he had left Bracebridge to return to work. I checked my watch. It was well past the time he typically came home from the bakery. I called his phone but it went directly to voicemail. There was no way I was going to leave a message: *Hey, Bear. Small problem. I neglected to tell you your girlfriend has been bonking your roommate and the two are running off to California with your hard-earned cash. Talk to you later.* Instead, I simply said, "It's Pen, give me a call." Then I made a promise to explain everything the moment he called back.

I thought about my short tenure at Honest Ed's. I had quit two jobs in one summer. It was so unlike me. I emptied my refrigerator into a cooler and carried my belongings to the car. I knocked once more at Bear's door but there was still no answer. Finally, I locked my apartment and stuck a post-dated rent cheque in the super's mail slot. I would return.

Thirty-Nine

Hospital visiting hours were over when I snuck into my father's room. He had been moved into a ward with three other men. One wizened old man winked at me as I crossed the room. I peeked behind the curtains encircling my father's bed.

My mouth dropped open. Bear was sitting on a visitor chair, his feet propped up on the bed. My father was eating Ben and Jerry's ice cream out of the carton.

"Are you allowed to eat that?" I asked.

Bear swung his feet to the floor.

"Back on solids," my father said. A bowl of Jello and a cup of bouillon sat untouched on the tray before him.

"Isn't this a work day for you?" I asked Bear.

He folded a paper and tucked it into the pocket of a cowboy shirt. "Can't a dude do a good deed without getting the fifth degree?"

"The fifth what?" Dad asked, looking back and forth between the two of us.

Bear stood up. "I'll leave you to visit with your daughter." He shook my dad's hand. "Adios."

My father had a goofy expression plastered on his face; I wrote it off as a reaction to the medication. Maybe I should ask Kim to get the doctors to reduce his meds.

"I really appreciate how you kids are helping me out," he said. "Especially Bear coming all the way from Toronto."

I eyed him incredulously. When I pulled the chair close to the bed, he looked like he wanted to say something more. I waited, but he continued to eat the ice cream.

"Do you want to hear some excerpts from my body image interviews?" I asked." I'm almost finished my article."

"Sure," he mouthed, licking the spoon.

After I had read a few pages, he put his hand on mine. "It's very good. You have to finish it," he said. "Why not submit it to the paper here?"

"I'm not staying long term. You know that." I shoved my notebook into my bag.

My father pressed the down button for the head of the bed, closing his eyes. "How about showing it to Bob Mac-Kenzie? He'll give you some good direction."

Bob MacKenzie owned the local paper and was the father of my archenemies, the MacKenzie sisters. In contrast to his daughters, and my ex-boss, I liked his manner. He was approachable.

I had lots of time on my hands, so the next morning I decided to take my father's advice. I would try to find Bear afterwards.

I walked up the steps of the newspaper office. From the hallway, I could see Bob Mac-Kenzie eating a tuna sandwich at his desk. His door was open.

"Hey, Pen," he said, looking up. He offered me half of his sandwich. "Sorry to hear about your dad. How's he feeling?"

"Getting stronger every day," I replied.

I pitched the theme and intent of my story. I showed him my interview notes, and asked if he might consider it for a freelance article. He leaned forward, elbows on his desk pad. Writers are wired for refusals. So I steadied myself, ready for rejection. Perhaps the article was really geared for a national periodical, rather than a small-town newspaper.

"You polish it up and I'll definitely consider it for a feature in one of our weekend editions. It's about time you were writing more serious material."

"I'll have it to you by next week, Bob. And thank you." I felt my heart pounding in my throat. In disbelief, I collected my papers and shoved them into my backpack.

"Give your father my best," he said, folding his sandwich paper. "I heard he's closing the restaurant down for a while."

"What?" I stood up.

"You didn't know?"

I shook my head.

"Marge at the bank told me he's taking on a partner."

I was confounded. Why hadn't Dad mentioned something so important? I couldn't believe Marlin had agreed to be a partner. And why close the business down? It didn't make sense. "I was at the hospital a few minutes ago — Marge must be confused. Marlin and I are running the place until my dad's back on his feet." I reached over the desk to shake his hand, and as I did, noticed my ex-boss pass by the office door. His bony jaw dropped when he saw me.

Leaving my car parked on the main street, I slowly walked to the restaurant. I needed a few minutes to think. Only a few days ago, my brother and I had agreed to band together to temporarily keep the family business afloat. Hadn't I just left my job in the city? I stood outside the door for a second, feeling increasingly irate.

The breakfast rush was over. Only two women remained, chatting over mugs of coffee. Itsy was bussing tables. She smiled at me as I walked past her and into the kitchen. Bear was chopping onions and Marlin was cleaning the grill. Both glanced up as I slammed the kitchen door behind me.

"What the heck is going on?" I asked my brother. "And what are you doing here?" I stabbed a finger in Bear's direction. "I was just at the newspaper office and Mr. MacKenzie told me you're closing down the restaurant." Marlin stopped scraping the blackened stove.

"Bear, you better get her up to speed," he said tossing down the spatula and disappearing into the dining room.

I felt frustrated and outraged. I smoothed my shirt and turned to Bear. His happy grin matched my father's earlier elation. Then I suddenly remembered his situation, the terrible Giselle and her new lover. Whatever else happened during this conversation, Bear deserved some respect and kindness.

I put up my hand. "Let me speak first," I announced. "I've kept quiet way too long. I went for a midnight stroll last week in Toronto."

Bear raised his bushy eyebrows.

"I was upset." I began to ramble. "There was this car and it chased me down a dark alley. I jumped over a fence into a backyard." I paused again. "The point is, when I returned to the apartment and was about to cross the street, I caught sight of Giselle and Lucas."

Bear had put down the knife down on the counter to listen to me. He growled. I looked up. And then his snarl erupted into laughter. "Other than Jake, I knew you were all jacked up about something that night we went to Hamilton. Is this what you were afraid to tell me?"

"I was going to tell you right after we found Jake. It was completely selfish of me to not disclose what I knew sooner. But then…" My voice petered out.

He grabbed my hand. "I left her."

"What?"

"I came home that day after driving you to the hospital and I told her I could no longer be with her because…"

I interrupted, pulling my hand away. "She stole your life savings?"

He shook his head.

"Oh, thank God. I swear I would have hunted her down single-handedly if she had taken your start-up money!"

Marlin poked his head through the door. "Did you tell her yet?"

"Tell me what?' I snapped. I wasn't sure whether I was prepared to hear anything more. I was exhausted.

Bear motioned for me to follow him into my father's office. We sat on opposite sides of the desk.

"You know how I told you I wanted to run my own business," he explained.

I nodded. My thoughts spun, doing double time. Had Dad and Marlin sold the restaurant? Not Bear? Was he going to change it into a bakery?

"My father drove up here yesterday," he said.

I stood up. "What's going on here and why am I the last to know?"

"Sit down and I'll tell you," urged Bear.

I crossed my arms, shook my head and sat down.

"Don't look as if I've just murdered your grandmother," he said. "Relax, this is good news. My parents are loaning me money to partner with your dad in a business venture.

We're going upscale in a new location. I'll be running the bakery side, baking bread and desserts for the restaurant, as well as selling to other eateries and grocery stores. Your dad has already started planning the menu. No more burgers and fries." His eyes flashed with excitement. "Boyd is designing the new dining room and Marlin has agreed to build it."

"Why didn't anyone tell me?" I said bitterly. "Why did you all go behind my back?"

"I swear to God, it virtually happened overnight," Bear insisted. "I called in sick yesterday and drove to Bracebridge to tell you about Giselle. I didn't know you were on your way back to the apartment. On the drive north, an idea hit me. There was no reason to tie myself to Toronto. I thought about how your dad needs help, how his business could be so much more. He's an amazing chef and he's wasting his talents on meatloaf. And I'm a pretty good baker, doing mass cookie production. When I arrived at the hospital, Marlin and Itsy were in his room. I started blurting out this scheme. Everyone went crazy, yelling out ideas. A nurse had to tell us to be quiet or leave. Your dad said he felt like his stitches healed overnight."

I sat quietly — stunned. On the surface, it seemed to be the perfect solution. It would give Itsy a better job. Marlin would gain more experience at carpentry, not to mention allowing Boyd's design abilities to flourish — a real family affair. And it would let me off the hook. I could return to the city, work on my writing, get the article published, send out more resumes and pursue my career in journalism.

Just one thing. Why was I feeling like an outsider? Perhaps it was because this man I hardly knew was flying in like a superhero to save the day. And there was no room for me.

Bear continued to ramble. "My father arrived and immediately hit it off with your dad. He's coming up next week with my mother. They're going to be silent partners, but they want to meet everyone."

"Sounds just grand," I whispered, looking down.

"Pen," said Bear, "What's the matter? Is it Jake? I know the other night must have been devastating. You haven't had time to assimilate that, let alone your dad's operation and every else that's been happening." Suddenly, he looked concerned and sad.

Part of me wanted to collapse into his arms, but instead, I bolted out of my father's chair, pushed past a confused Marlin, who was lurking by the freezer, and ran out the back door of the restaurant. My car was blocks away. I heard Bear behind me. I rushed around the side of the building and just then, Kim pulled up in her car. I opened the passenger side door, dove in and yelled, "Drive!"

Forty

Kim shot into traffic, narrowly missing a pickup truck. "Who's chasing you?" she asked, glancing into the rear-view mirror. I turned around to look and saw Bear standing stoically on the sidewalk, staring intently at us as we drove away.

"How long have you known about the restaurant?" I demanded.

"Only since yesterday. They asked Boyd to come to the hospital to talk about the design." She didn't seem to notice my outrage. She honked at a car that cut in front of us. "Isn't it exciting?" she exclaimed. "He's at home right now working away at his drafting table, whistling and singing those infuriating *Jesus Christ Superstar* songs."

"Am I the very last to know?" I fumed.

Kim looked over at me. "Sometimes, Pen, you're so melodramatic."

"Pull over!" I yelled. Even my best friend didn't understand. "I'm such bad luck that even my family doesn't want me involved."

"What in the world are you talking about?" She swung into the drug store parking lot and shut off the engine. "You think you're a jinx?"

"You're so in love with Boyd—your life is eternal bliss," I said.

"For heaven's sake," said Kim, grabbing me by the collar. "Sometimes I could shake the living daylights out of you. When will you stop seeing yourself as such a loser? And stop imagining that everyone else does too?"

Bear banged both hands down on the hood of the car. His face was beet red, sweat dripping off his forehead. He had chased us down the road on foot. Kim threw open the car door. "I have to pick up something in the drug store," she said, escaping into the parking lot.

Bear dove into the driver's seat. He was panting heavily, gulping to catch his breath.

"I'm so confused and angry, I don't know if I can talk to you or anyone right now," I said. "Here's a question. What could possibly have attracted you to Giselle in the first place? I need to know."

Bear inhaled deeply and then managed an answer. "Misguided reasons."

"What does that mean exactly?" I asked.

"My friends thought she was striking; therefore, I thought if I went out with her, my stock would go up. But..." Bear paused.

I interrupted. "Did you love her?"

"I thought I did," he responded. "But in retrospect, I was in love with being in love with her."

"What's wrong with us?" I said burying my head in my hands. "I've finally realized that Jake completely used me. At the beginning, I worshipped him and he seemed to be good to me. But when I think back, that only lasted a short time. It was me propping him up. Everything was all about him. A relationship can't be that one-sided and survive. It wasn't all my fault. And look at you and Giselle. She wanted to mould you into something you're not, and you put up with it. What a pair we are!"

He touched my arm. "Two peas in a shooter."

"If it weren't for bad luck, I'd have no luck at all," I retorted, crossing my arms.

He put his arm around my shoulder. "Misery loves company."

"And you have a face only a mother could love," I quipped.

"Well," he said, beaming. "My love for you is as plain as the nose on your face."

I stuck out my tongue. He leaned over to kiss me.

I pushed him away. "C'mon, Bear. We're just friends."

Forty-One

Kim looked surprised to see me sitting alone. I asked her to drop me off at my car. When we started moving, she threw a paper bag into my lap. "You can open it," she said. Inside were three brands of pregnancy tests.

"So you think you might be pregnant?" I uttered.

Kim nodded, her face aglow.

"I thought you applied to medical school?"

"I nixed that idea. My first instinct was correct. I like being a nurse. For a while I thought I just wasn't ambitious enough and should become a physician like my parents. Boyd helped me realize that I should set my own goals and be true to who I am and what I want. Maybe it's time to start a family," she ventured, smiling.

I drove home slowly. No one was at the house except Ziska, and even she seemed dejected. The place was empty, even emptier than after my mother's death. At least then we were together as a family, wrapped in our grief. Now I felt strangely disconnected from my brother and my father. My clothes and bags were still in the trunk. If Dad hadn't been in the hospital, I would have headed back to the city right then.

I was never a person to cry. I had learned how to bite my lip or jab my fingernails into my palms to stop the tears, a childhood talent born from not letting schoolyard bullies see me break. I had always been in control. My mother's death had shattered me but I had stood my ground, holding myself together for my father and brother. I was considered the strong one. Even after the Jake episode, there had been no tears in his honour. I was unlucky but damn it, I had always been a survivor.

But today, I sank to the floor where my mother's chair used to be and wept uncontrollably. I tried to stop. I chastised myself for giving in, and that made it worse. Tears rolled down my cheeks onto my shirt. Ziska hovered beside me, as still as a Buddha.

I didn't hear the car, nor the squeaky screen door opening. Ziska didn't even snarl. Suddenly I felt someone's arms around me, warm and comforting. I opened one eye, but I knew who it was. Neither of us spoke. I shuddered, hiccupping. Funny thing was I didn't feel any need to talk or explain. It was as if there was a radar-like symbiotic communication between us. Bear lay down on the floor with his legs and arms cradling me. For the first time in a long time, I felt safe.

In those moments that followed, I realized something about our relationship. We always had fun together. We were relaxed. I never had nervous tension or feelings of not being quite up to snuff when I was with Bear. There was nothing to prove. I realized that this was what a partnership should be all about. Neither one of us had ulterior motives; we simply enjoyed each other's company and our mutual wacky sense of humour. It may not have been love at first sight—I smile when I think about how quirky I found him at first. But I had to admit that recently, I had even started to look at him differently physically. Just when had that happened?

I wiped my eyes and my nose on my t-shirt, noticing an object on the floor beside us and an envelope sticking out of his pocket. "What's that?" I asked.

"It's for you," he said, handing me the thick packet. "An airline ticket to Ireland."

I pushed his hand away. "Come on, I can't accept this."

He sat up and reached for the object wrapped in my mother's linen tablecloth. "You left someone under the front seat of my car."

I gasped. When we had been out to see Marlin and the new shed, I had taken my mother from the closet and tucked her under the seat of his Oldsmobile. Then I had forgotten about her entirely.

"I kept hearing a voice," Bear said. "*Take my daughter to Ireland. She's never been to Dingle, Derry or Dublin.*" With that, he handed me her small box of ashes. "I thought I must be going barmy," he confessed.

He then slowly rose to his knees. "Will you marry me and become Mrs. Truman Berrington the Third?"

I sat up, getting to my knees, trembling, and uttered, "Yes. And absolutely no."

He looked perplexed.

"I will marry you, but I will not change my name to Penelope-Marie Berrington."

"Good enough," he replied, tenderly kissing me and brushing the hair gently off my face.

"On second thought, maybe it would make a great pen name for my first book," I whispered in his ear.

Epilogue

We decided against having a double wedding. No one does that, except in the movies. Itsy and Marlin wanted to wait and tie the knot in the spring, after *The Bear and the Fish* restaurant opened. Marlin grinned and said that it would give him time to find a good caterer for the reception.

Bear and I were married the weekend after Thanksgiving. A Justice of the Peace officiated on the front porch of Marlin's new shed. He and Itsy had installed the doors and windows. They had painted the board and batten Williamsburg blue with white trim. The weather co-operated and it didn't snow. Kim had been disappointed that we wouldn't delay the wedding until she could wear a maternity outfit to the affair.

I invited Jake's mother, but she declined. Mr. MacKenzie came, but without his notorious daughters. He had published my article and hired me back, promising blithely that I only had to report on class picnics sporadically. I was astonished to receive a bag of letters and hundreds of emails from women wanting to tell me their stories. Bear is now encouraging me to write that book.

We left right away for Dublin. At the top of Bear's list was kissing the Blarney Stone. I told him there was no way I was going to hang upside down to kiss a stone. Besides, I didn`t need to add the gift of gab to my repertoire. In a small makeup bag, I carried a little pouch of my mother's ashes disguised as face powder. I hoped when we passed through security at the airport they wouldn't stop the belt and rummage through my suitcase. They didn't, and my Mom is now laid to rest in the beautiful country she loved.

So, is fate predetermined, or do we make our own luck? As a child, I used to think people were marked at birth by some rubber-stamping god-like bureaucrat. Lucky. Unlucky. Lucky. Lucky. Somewhat lucky.

This past year I've begun to understand that we all have a lot more control over our destiny — our own luck, both good and bad — than we think. I fuelled my passion for writing, and look what happened.

I learned the hard way, and am still learning, not to let other people define who I am. Bear has taught me that healthy relationships can only happen when you truly learn to accept and love yourself. And beauty — well, I now realize it is definitely in the eye of the beholder.

Lucky or unlucky? These days, I think I'm one of the luckiest girls in Muskoka!

Made in the USA
Lexington, KY
14 May 2018